Political Extremism
in the United States

Other Books in the Current Controversies Series

Are There Two Americas?
The Confederate Flag
Deporting Immigrants
The Energy Industry
Enhanced Interrogation and Torture
Executive Orders
Freedom of Speech on Campus
Microaggressions, Safe Spaces, and Trigger Warnings
Police Training and Excessive Force
States' Rights and the Role of the Federal Government
Universal Health Care

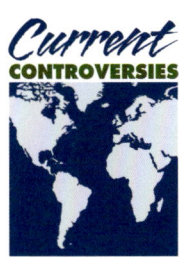

Political Extremism in the United States

Eamon Doyle, Book Editor

Published in 2019 by Greenhaven Publishing, LLC
353 3rd Avenue, Suite 255, New York, NY 10010

Copyright © 2019 by Greenhaven Publishing, LLC

First Edition

All rights reserved. No part of this book may be reproduced in any form without permission in writing from the publisher, except by a reviewer.

Articles in Greenhaven Publishing anthologies are often edited for length to meet page requirements. In addition, original titles of these works are changed to clearly present the main thesis and to explicitly indicate the author's opinion. Every effort is made to ensure that Greenhaven Publishing accurately reflects the original intent of the authors. Every effort has been made to trace the owners of the copyrighted material.

Cover image: Chip Somodevilla/Getty Images

Cataloging-in-Publication Data

Names: Doyle, Eamon, editor.
Title: Political extremism in the United States / edited by Eamon Doyle.
Description: New York : Greenhaven Publishing, 2019. | Series: Current controversies | Includes bibliographical references and index. | Audience: Grades 9–12.
Identifiers: LCCN ISBN 9781534503106 (library bound) | ISBN 9781534503113 (pbk.)
Subjects: LCSH: Radicalism—Juvenile literature. | United States—Politics and government—21st century—Juvenile literature.
Classification: LCC HN49.R33 P655 2019 | DDC 303.48/4—dc23

Manufactured in the United States of America

Website: http://greenhavenpublishing.com

Contents

Foreword   11
Introduction   15

Chapter 1: Does Political Extremism Play a Positive Role in American Democracy?

Extremism and Polarization in America Spring from a Complex Confluence of Cultural, Discursive, and Political Dynamics   20

Lumen Learning

There is no single primary cause of political polarization and extremist rhetoric in politics. A number of deeply embedded dynamics factor into political extremism.

Yes: Conflict Is Good for Democracy and Shows that Citizens Are Engaged

American Politics Benefit from the Energy and Intensity of Extremism   31

Trevor Whitney

The ossification and intransigence in American politics today reflects the lack of ideological distinction between the parties. American democracy depends on clear choices, which is the often unnoticed benefit of extremist politics.

Extremism Is Difficult to Define and Difficult to Restrict Without Curtailing Freedom of Expression in General   34

Courtney Radsch

Despite the drawbacks of extremism in politics, it serves a purpose by giving voice to uncommon perspectives. Furthermore, it would be difficult to eradicate extremist rhetoric without fundamentally altering American norms around free speech and freedom of the press.

No: A Mature Democracy Should Be Driven by a Thoughtful, Well-Ordered Exchange of Views

Democracy Should Be Oriented Toward Reasoned Deliberation and Consensus, Not Conflict and Extremism
39

Robert E. Ferrell and Joe Old

The authors examine conflict in American politics through the lens of Jürgen Habermas's theory of discourse ethics and deliberative communication.

The Electoral Layer of Democracy Lends Itself to Extremist Politics, Which Threatens the Governing Layer of Democracy
45

Amy Gutmann and Dennis Thompson

Extremist rhetoric can help candidates gain an edge in a campaign, but running the government requires coalition-building and compromise. The increasing influence of campaign strategy on daily government affairs has allowed intransigent, oppositional mindsets to disrupt a discursive space that thrives on compromise.

Chapter 2: Do Political Parties Promote Extremism?

Political Parties in the United States Play a Major Role in Framing Key Political Issues and Structuring Public Opinion
56

Delia Baldassarri and Andrew Gelman

The history of American politics shows that parties affect both the content and the temper of public sentiment. Extreme rhetoric can spring from tension in the alignment between parties.

Yes: Especially in a Dual System, Political Parties Tend to Entrench Ideological Divisions and Promote Extremist and Antagonistic Rhetoric

Party-Based Political Gridlock Interferes with Rational Dialogue on Key Issues
76

Jack Zhou

When political parties organize themselves around key issues (such as the Republican Party's skepticism toward climate change), party identification can stand in the way of efforts to achieve bipartisan consensus.

A Diverse Society Like the United States Needs More Than Two Political Parties 82

Kristin Eberhard

At a time when fewer and fewer Americans identify with the two major political parties, the introduction of a competitive third party would energize the system and hopefully provide a mainstream voice for alienated, disenfranchised citizens.

Political Extremism Is an Ingrained Part of the American Political System 92

Michael Atkinson and Daniel Béland

The institutional design of the United States government—the separation of powers, the dual party system—tends to encourage extremist politics.

No: Political Parties Are a Necessary Structural Aspect of Any Functioning Democracy

Strong and Stable Political Parties Are Essential to the Health of American Democracy 99

Richard H. Pildes

American democracy depends on a careful balance between the dynamism of popular participation and the restraining structure of political parties.

Political Parties Guard Against the Risks of Popular Democratic Governance 119

Democracy Web

Classical political philosophers such as John Stuart Mill understood the important role that political parties play in a democracy. The fundamental dynamics of this relationship have endured throughout history.

Chapter 3: Have the Dynamics of Contemporary Media Contributed to Extremism?

The Contemporary News Media Environment Raises Questions About How Networks Use Extreme Rhetoric to Attract Audiences 128

Alex Slack

The competitive dynamics of the news business have led to a more diverse and fragmented media landscape. This in turn has led to a tension between traditional editorial goals—such as accuracy and transparency—and the pressure to produce profits.

Yes: To Attract and Maintain the Attention of Their Audience, Editors and Reporters Often Focus on the Loudest, Most Extreme Political Actors

Media Diversification Has Led to a New Business Model Where Sources Compete for the Loyalty of Small, Ideologically Defined Demographics   131

Shelley Hepworth

News sources that conform their coverage to the ideology of a partisan market have raised the temperature of public debate by amplifying extreme voices and focusing on conflict.

The History of Fox News Illustrates How and Why the Contemporary Media Landscape Came to Embrace Ideologically Structured Coverage   136

David Folkenflik

The Fox News Network exemplifies how media organizations have capitalized on political polarization and ideological conflict in American society, and how this type of coverage works to reinforce those dynamics.

Media Outlets Are Focused on Attracting Attention, Not Informing the Public   144

Ben Gerow

Traditional media outlets are struggling to survive, and in order to stay afloat they amplify the loudest voices in the room. This encourages their audience to pay attention to extreme voices rather than reasoned, balanced takes on current events.

No: The Polarization of American Politics Reflects a Set of Institutional and Cultural Dynamics that Transcend the Current Media Environment

Extremism and Demagoguery Emerge from Social Dynamics that Have Little to Do with Media Coverage   149

Larry Diamond

Extremism has a long history in modern American politics. There are deep ideological fissures in American society that stretch back to the Vietnam era and McCarthyism. The contemporary media environment might exacerbate these dynamics, but it did not create them.

The Media Is Beholden to the Political Forces at Play   155

Indira Lakshmanan

While many considered the far-right news website Breitbart News to be a driving force behind President Trump's election, in reality media outlets like Breitbart are beholden to a variety of political forces. These include political interest groups, which help fund media outlets, as well as the president himself, who controls the amount of access granted to the media.

Chapter 4: Has the Internet and Its Growing Role in Society Contributed to Political Extremism?

The Power of Social Media and the Internet Has Created Opportunities and Perils for Society   164

Clay Shirky

Healthy normative restraints can help us to avoid the worst effects of social media and the internet while drawing on their capacity to connect people and to energize democracy.

Yes: Social Media and the Internet Have Directly Contributed to Paranoia and Extremism in American Politics

The Rapid, 24/7 News Cycle Made Possible by Modern Media Technology Has Diminished the Depth and Quality of Public Discourse   170

Ben Harack

As media outlets compete to provide real-time and exclusive coverage, speed and efficiency have displaced traditional journalistic goals such as accuracy, verification, and transparency.

Social Media and the Internet Have Failed to Mitigate Persistent Class-Based Gaps in Political Participation   174

Marc Hooghe, Jennifer Oser, and Sofie Marien

Popular arguments suggest that social media has the potential to draw previously disengaged populations (such as low-income and less educated individuals) into the political process. The data, however, tells a different story.

Confirmation Bias Threatens the Potential Benefits of a Diverse Media Environment   177

Martin Maximino

Research shows that media consumers, when faced with a diverse, competitive media landscape, tend to gravitate toward coverage that reinforces their own cultural and ideological biases.

No: The Internet Has Allowed for Candidates and Elected Officials to Communicate More Directly with the Public, Increasing Political Engagement

Citizens Who Consume More Media Are More Politically Engaged   181

John Wihbey

Recent studies have suggested that heavy news consumers tend to be better informed and more politically active than those who consume less news media.

Social Media Offers New Tools for Political Engagement   184

Deana A. Rohlinger

Examples including hashtag campaigns, virtual petitions, and online money-bombs show how social media has opened up new avenues of political participation, which have empowered citizens and shaped new political movements.

Organizations to Contact   188
Bibliography   192
Index   195

Foreword

"Controversy" is a word that has an undeniably unpleasant connotation. It carries a definite negative charge. Controversy can spoil family gatherings, spread a chill around classroom and campus discussion, inflame public discourse, open raw civic wounds, and lead to the ouster of public officials. We often feel that controversy is almost akin to bad manners, a rude and shocking eruption of that which must not be spoken or thought of in polite, tightly guarded society. To avoid controversy, to quell controversy, is often seen as a public good, a victory for etiquette, perhaps even a moral or ethical imperative.

Yet the studious, deliberate avoidance of controversy is also a whitewashing, a denial, a death threat to democracy. It is a false sterilizing and sanitizing and superficial ordering of the messy, ragged, chaotic, at times ugly processes by which a healthy democracy identifies and confronts challenges, engages in passionate debate about appropriate approaches and solutions, and arrives at something like a consensus and a broadly accepted and supported way forward. Controversy is the megaphone, the speaker's corner, the public square through which the citizenry finds and uses its voice. Controversy is the life's blood of our democracy and absolutely essential to the vibrant health of our society.

Our present age is certainly no stranger to controversy. We are consumed by fierce debates about technology, privacy, political correctness, poverty, violence, crime and policing, guns, immigration, civil and human rights, terrorism, militarism, environmental protection, and gender and racial equality. Loudly competing voices are raised every day, shouting opposing opinions, putting forth competing agendas, and summoning starkly different visions of a utopian or dystopian future. Often these voices attempt to shout the others down; there is precious little listening and considering among the cacophonous din. Yet listening and considering, too, are essential to the health of a democracy. If controversy is democracy's lusty lifeblood, respectful listening and careful thought are its higher faculties, its brain, its conscience.

Current Controversies does not shy away from or attempt to hush the loudly competing voices. It seeks to provide readers with as wide and representative as possible a range of articulate voices on any given controversy of the day, separates each one out to allow it to be heard clearly and fairly, and encourages careful listening to each of these well-crafted, thoughtfully expressed opinions, supplied by some of today's leading academics, thinkers, analysts, politicians, policy makers, economists, activists, change agents, and advocates. Only after listening to a wide range of opinions on an issue, evaluating the strengths and weaknesses of each argument, assessing how well the facts and available evidence mesh with the stated opinions and conclusions, and thoughtfully and critically examining one's own beliefs and conscience can the reader begin to arrive at his or her own conclusions and articulate his or her own stance on the spotlighted controversy.

This process is facilitated and supported in each *Current Controversies* volume by an introduction and chapter overviews that provide readers with the essential context they need to begin engaging with the spotlighted controversies, with the debates surrounding them, and with their own perhaps shifting or nascent opinions on them. Chapters are organized around several key questions that are answered with diverse opinions representing all points on the political spectrum. In its content, organization, and methodology, readers are encouraged to determine the authors' point of view and purpose, interrogate and analyze the various arguments and their rhetoric and structure, evaluate the arguments' strengths and weaknesses, test their claims against available facts and evidence, judge the validity of the reasoning, and bring into clearer, sharper focus the reader's own beliefs and conclusions and how they may differ from or align with those in the collection or those of classmates.

Research has shown that reading comprehension skills improve dramatically when students are provided with compelling, intriguing, and relevant "discussable" texts. The subject matter of these collections could not be more compelling, intriguing, or urgently relevant to today's students and the world they are poised to inherit. The anthologized articles also provide the basis for stimulating, lively, and passionate classroom debates. Students who are compelled to anticipate objections to their own argument and identify the flaws in those of an opponent read more carefully, think more critically, and steep themselves in relevant context, facts, and information more thoroughly. In short, using discussable text of the kind provided by every single volume in the *Current Controversies* series encourages close reading, facilitates reading comprehension, fosters research, strengthens critical thinking, and greatly enlivens and energizes classroom discussion and participation. The entire learning process is deepened, extended, and strengthened.

If we are to foster a knowledgeable, responsible, active, and engaged citizenry, we must provide readers with the intellectual, interpretive, and critical-thinking tools and experience necessary to make sense of the world around them and of the all-important debates and arguments that inform it. We must encourage them not to run away from or attempt to quell controversy but to embrace it in a responsible, conscientious, and thoughtful way, to sharpen and strengthen their own informed opinions by listening to and critically analyzing those of others. This series encourages respectful engagement with and analysis of current controversies and competing opinions and fosters a resulting increase in the strength and rigor of one's own opinions and stances. As such, it helps readers assume their rightful place in the public square and provides them with the skills necessary to uphold their awesome responsibility—guaranteeing the continued and future health of a vital, vibrant, and free democracy.

Introduction

> *By all conventional measures, the parties in government are more polarized than at any time since the late nineteenth century. But keep in mind that partisan polarization is not necessarily bad, or all bad, from a broader democratic perspective.* [1]
>
> -Richard H. Pildes

Political values and policy platforms are often measured on a continuum from moderate to extreme. A moderate (or "centrist") political perspective is usually characterized by wide agreement with prevailing ideologies, an openness to compromise, and a willingness to incorporate good ideas that come from a variety of viewpoints, rather than drawing exclusively from a single specific ideology. On the other hand, extremist perspectives (sometimes referred to as "radical") generally reject important aspects of prevailing cultural ideologies, are less inclined to compromise, and are based around an allegiance to a specific ideology or belief system (liberal, socialist, conservative, libertarian, etc.).

In electoral democracies with bipolar or multipolar party systems, the moderate-extreme continuum is usually applied based on party platforms. For instance, a conservative party may have a number of moderate members who largely align with the platform but who are interested in pursuing pragmatic, uncontroversial policies, and in a bipartisan or multipartisan fashion when possible. Extremist members of the same party would, on the other hand, adopt a dogmatic attitude toward the party platform and discourage compromise and bipartisanship in favor of aggressive and transformative policies.

To some degree, extremism in politics derives from the distinct imperatives of governing and campaigning:

> To campaign successfully, politicians must mobilize and inspire their supporters. They have to articulate a coherent vision distinct from that of their opponents, and present their opponents as adversaries to be mistrusted and ultimately defeated. But to govern effectively, politicians must find ways to reach agreements with their opponents, including members of their own ideologically diverse parties—even some compromises that their own supporters may see as betrayals. This tension between what is required in a democracy to win power and what is required to exercise it is manifest in what we have called uncompromising and compromising mindsets. These two clusters of attitudes and arguments arise from the distinctions between the pressures of democratic campaigning and those of governing, and they frame the way politicians and the public view the opportunities for and the outcomes of compromises. [2]

This perspective locates the causes of extremism in the institutions and procedures that comprise democratic politics.

Other writers have adopted a perspective on political extremism more focused on deep-rooted cultural dynamics and social or communication norms. In a diverse society like the United States, factors like economic inequality and persistent racism can push various interest and identity groups to distrust each other on a level that transcends the vagaries of electoral politics. The political theorist Amy Gutmann describes the risks of extremist rhetoric:

> In a democracy, controversy is healthy. Complex issues as far-ranging as immigration, health care, military interventions, taxation, and education seldom lend themselves to simple, consensual solutions. The public interest is well served by robust

public argument. But when disagreements are so driven and distorted by extremist rhetoric that citizens and public officials fail to engage with one another reasonably or respectfully on substantive issues of public importance, the debate degenerates, blocking constructive compromises that would benefit all sides more than the status quo would.[3]

Whether one adopts an institutional/procedural or a social/cultural framework, it is easy to see why political theorists regard extremism as an important factor in determining the health of a democracy.

From another direction, many writers have argued that changes in the news business and in the media landscape overall have contributed to extremism and polarization in American politics. In the middle of the twentieth century, most Americans received their news from local papers and a small handful of national broadcasters. These sources, because they assumed they were communicating with a mass audience, were careful to avoid ideological bias in their coverage. But as the news media landscape diversified, mass-audience sources have been overwhelmed by a profusion of smaller-market publications that tailor coverage for specific, ideological demographics. While some have cheered the diversification of the media landscape, writers like Martin Maximino have suggested that confirmation bias encourages news consumers to seek coverage that reinforces and strengthens their own prejudices.[4]

Despite the various perspectives on what causes extremism, there is wide agreement among those who study democratic politics that extremism and polarization are among the most important and consequential political dynamics in the United States today. The viewpoints presented in *Current Controversies: Political Extremism in the United States* explore the nature of American extremism and explain potential ways to either combat or harness it for the benefit of the country.

Political Extremism in the United States

Notes

1. "Romanticizing Democracy, Political Fragmentation, and the Decline of American Government," by Richard H. Pildes, The Yale Law Journal, December 2014.

2. "The Mindsets of Political Compromise," by Amy Gutmann and Dennis Thompson, University Of Pennsylvania.

3. "The Lure & Dangers of Extremist Rhetoric," by Amy Gutmann, University of Pennsylvania, 2007.

4. "Does media fragmentation contribute to polarization? Evidence from lab experiments," by Martin Maximino, Journalist's Resource, August 22, 2014. https://journalistsresource.org/studies/society/news-media/media-fragmentation-political-polarization-lab-experiments.

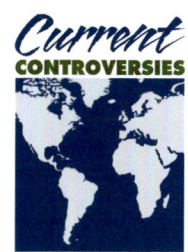

Chapter 1

| Does Political Extremism Play a Positive Role in American Democracy?

Extremism and Polarization in America Spring from a Complex Confluence of Cultural, Discursive, and Political Dynamics

Lumen Learning

Lumen Learning's mission is to make great learning opportunities available to all students, regardless of socioeconomic background. They accomplish this by using open educational resources (OER) to create well-designed and low-cost course materials that replace expensive textbooks.

The past thirty years have brought a dramatic change in the relationship between the two parties as fewer conservative Democrats and liberal Republicans have been elected to office. As political moderates, or individuals with ideologies in the middle of the ideological spectrum, leave the political parties at all levels, the parties have grown farther apart ideologically, a result called party polarization. In other words, at least organizationally and in government, Republicans and Democrats have become increasingly dissimilar from one another. In the party-in-government, this means fewer members of Congress have mixed voting records; instead they vote far more consistently on issues and are far more likely to side with their party leadership.[1]

It also means a growing number of moderate voters aren't participating in party politics. Either they are becoming independents, or they are participating only in the general election and are therefore not helping select party candidates in primaries.

What is most interesting about this shift to increasingly polarized parties is that it does not appear to have happened as a result of the structural reforms recommended by APSA. Rather,

---

"Divided Government and Partisan Polarization," Lumen Learning. https://courses.lumenlearning.com/amgovernment/chapter/divided-government-and-partisan-polarization/. Licensed under CC BY 4.0 International.

it has happened because moderate politicians have simply found it harder and harder to win elections. There are many conflicting theories about the causes of polarization, some of which we discuss below. But whatever its origin, party polarization in the United States does not appear to have had the net positive effects that the APSA committee was hoping for. With the exception of providing voters with more distinct choices, positives of polarization are hard to find. The negative impacts are many. For one thing, rather than reducing interparty conflict, polarization appears to have only amplified it. For example, the Republican Party (or the GOP, standing for Grand Old Party) has historically been a coalition of two key and overlapping factions: pro-business rightists and social conservatives. The GOP has held the coalition of these two groups together by opposing programs designed to redistribute wealth (and advocating small government) while at the same time arguing for laws preferred by conservative Christians. But it was also willing to compromise with pro-business Democrats, often at the expense of social issues, if it meant protecting long-term business interests.

Recently, however, a new voice has emerged that has allied itself with the Republican Party. Born in part from an older third-party movement known as the Libertarian Party, the Tea Party is more hostile to government and views government intervention in all forms, and especially taxation and the regulation of business, as a threat to capitalism and democracy. It is less willing to tolerate interventions in the market place, even when they are designed to protect the markets themselves. Although an anti-tax faction within the Republican Party has existed for some time, some factions of the Tea Party movement are also active at the intersection of religious liberty and social issues, especially in opposing such initiatives as same-sex marriage and abortion rights.[2] The Tea Party has argued that government, both directly and by neglect, is threatening the ability of evangelicals to observe their moral obligations, including practices some perceive as endorsing social exclusion.

Political Extremism in the United States

Although the Tea Party is a movement and not a political party, 86 percent of Tea Party members who voted in 2012 cast their votes for Republicans.[3] Some members of the Republican Party are closely affiliated with the movement, and before the 2012 elections, Tea Party activist Grover Norquist exacted promises from many Republicans in Congress that they would oppose any bill that sought to raise taxes.[4] The inflexibility of Tea Party members has led to tense floor debates and was ultimately responsible for the 2014 primary defeat of Republican majority leader Eric Cantor and the 2015 resignation of the sitting Speaker of the House John Boehner. In 2015, Chris Christie, John Kasich, Ben Carson, Marco Rubio, and Ted Cruz, all of whom were Republican presidential candidates, signed Norquist's pledge as well.

Movements on the left have also arisen. The Occupy Wall Street movement was born of the government's response to the Great Recession of 2008 and its assistance to endangered financial institutions, provided through the Troubled Asset Relief Program, TARP. The Occupy Movement believed the recession was caused by a failure of the government to properly regulate the banking industry. The Occupiers further maintained that the government moved swiftly to protect the banking industry from the worst of the recession but largely failed to protect the average person, thereby worsening the growing economic inequality in the United States.

While the Occupy Movement itself has largely fizzled, the anti-business sentiment to which it gave voice continues within the Democratic Party, and many Democrats have proclaimed their support for the movement and its ideals, if not for its tactics.[5] Champions of the left wing of the Democratic Party, however, such as presidential candidate Senator Bernie Sanders and Massachusetts Senator Elizabeth Warren, have ensured that the Occupy Movement's calls for more social spending and higher taxes on the wealthy remain a prominent part of the national debate. Their popularity, and the growing visibility of race issues in the United States, have helped sustain the left wing of the Democratic Party. Bernie Sanders' presidential run made these topics and causes even more salient, especially among younger voters. To date, however, the Occupy Movement has had fewer electoral effects than has the Tea Party. Yet, as manifested in Sanders' candidacy, it has the potential to affect races at lower levels in the 2016 national elections.

Unfortunately, party factions haven't been the only result of party polarization. By most measures, the US government in general and Congress in particular have become less effective in recent years. Congress has passed fewer pieces of legislation, confirmed fewer appointees, and been less effective at handling the national purse than in recent memory. If we define effectiveness as legislative productivity, the 106th Congress (1999–2000) passed 463 pieces of substantive legislation (not including commemorative legislation, such as bills proclaiming an official doughnut of the United States). The 107th Congress (2000–2001) passed 294 such pieces of legislation. By 2013–2014, the total had fallen to 212.[6]

Perhaps the clearest sign of Congress' ineffectiveness is that the threat of government shutdown has become a constant. Shutdowns occur when Congress and the president are unable to authorize and appropriate funds before the current budget runs out. This is now an annual problem. Relations between the two parties became so bad that financial markets were sent into turmoil in 2014 when Congress failed to increase the government's line of credit before a key deadline, thus threatening a US government default on its loans. While any particular trend can be the result of multiple factors, the decline of key measures of institutional confidence and trust suggest the negative impact of polarization. Public approval ratings for Congress have been near single digits for several years, and a poll taken in February 2016 revealed that only 11 percent of respondents thought Congress was doing a "good or excellent job."[7] President Obama's average approval rating has remained low, despite an overall trend of economic growth since the end of the 2008 recession.[8] Typically, economic conditions are a significant driver of presidential approval, suggesting the negative effect of partisanship on presidential approval.

The Causes of Polarization

Scholars agree that some degree of polarization is occurring in the United States, even if some contend it is only at the elite level. But they are less certain about exactly why, or how, polarization has become such a mainstay of American politics. Several conflicting theories have been offered. The first and perhaps best argument is that polarization is a party-in-government phenomenon driven by a decades-long sorting of the voting public, or a change in party allegiance in response to shifts in party position.[9] According to the sorting thesis, before the 1950s, voters were mostly concerned with state-level party positions rather than national party concerns. Since parties are bottom-up institutions, this meant local issues dominated elections; it also meant national-level politicians typically paid more attention to local problems than to national party politics.

But over the past several decades, voters have started identifying more with national-level party politics, and they began to demand their elected representatives become more attentive to national party positions. As a result, they have become more likely to pick parties that consistently represent national ideals, are more consistent in their candidate selection, and are more willing to elect office-holders likely to follow their party's national agenda. One example of the way social change led to party sorting revolves around race.

The Democratic Party returned to national power in the 1930s largely as the result of a coalition among low socio-economic status voters in northern and midwestern cities. These new Democratic voters were religiously and ethnically more diverse than the mostly white, mostly Protestant voters who supported Republicans. But the southern United States (often called the "Solid South") had been largely dominated by Democratic politicians since the Civil War. These politicians agreed with other Democrats on most issues, but they were more evangelical in their religious beliefs and less tolerant on racial matters. The federal nature of the United States meant that Democrats in other parts of the country were free to seek alliances with minorities in their states. But in the South, African Americans were still largely disenfranchised well after Franklin Roosevelt had brought other groups into the Democratic tent.

The Democratic alliance worked relatively well through the 1930s and 1940s when post-Depression politics revolved around supporting farmers and helping the unemployed. But in the late 1950s and early 1960s, social issues became increasingly prominent in national politics. Southern Democrats, who had supported giving the federal government authority for economic redistribution, began to resist calls for those powers to be used to restructure society. Many of these Democrats broke away from the party only to find a home among Republicans, who were willing to help promote smaller national government and greater states' rights.[10] This shift was largely completed with the rise of the evangelical movement in politics, when it shepherded its supporters away from Jimmy Carter, an evangelical Christian, to Ronald Reagan in the 1980 presidential election.

At the same time social issues were turning the Solid South towards the Republican Party, they were having the opposite effect in the North and West. Moderate Republicans, who had been champions of racial equality since the time of Lincoln, worked with Democrats to achieve social reform. These Republicans found it increasing difficult to remain in their party as it began to adjust to the growing power of the small government–states' rights movement. A good example was Senator Arlen Specter, a moderate Republican who represented Pennsylvania and ultimately switched to become a Democrat before the end of his political career.

A second possible culprit in increased polarization is the impact of technology on the public square. Before the 1950s, most people got their news from regional newspapers and local radio stations. While some national programming did exist, most editorial control was in the hands of local publishers and editorial boards. These groups served as a filter of sorts as they tried to meet the demands of local markets.

As described in detail in the media chapter, the advent of television changed that. Television was a powerful tool, with national news and editorial content that provided the same message across the country. All viewers saw the same images of the women's rights movement and the war in Vietnam. The expansion of news coverage to cable, and the consolidation of local news providers into big corporate conglomerates, amplified this nationalization. Average citizens were just as likely to learn what it meant to be a Republican from a politician in another state as from one in their own, and national news coverage made it much more difficult for politicians to run away from their votes. The information explosion that followed the heyday of network TV by way of cable, the Internet, and blogs has furthered this nationalization trend.

A final possible cause for polarization is the increasing sophistication of gerrymandering, or the manipulation of legislative districts in an attempt to favor a particular candidate. According to the gerrymandering thesis, the more moderate or heterogeneous a voting district, the more moderate the politician's behavior once in office. Taking extreme or one-sided positions on a large number of issues would be hazardous for a member who needs to build a diverse electoral coalition. But if the district has been drawn to favor a particular group, it now is necessary for the elected official to serve only the portion of the constituency that dominates.

Gerrymandering is a centuries-old practice. There has always been an incentive for legislative bodies to draw districts in such a way that sitting legislators have the best chance of keeping their jobs. But changes in law and technology have transformed gerrymandering from a crude art into a science. The first advance came with the introduction of the "one-person-one-vote" principle by the US Supreme Court in 1962. Before then, it was common for many states to practice redistricting, or redrawing of their electoral maps, *only* if they gained or lost seats in the US House of Representatives. This can happen once every ten years as a result of a constitutionally mandated reapportionment process, in which the number of House seats given to each state is adjusted to account for population changes.

But if there was no change in the number of seats, there was little incentive to shift district boundaries. After all, if a legislator had won election based on the current map, any change to the map could make losing seats more likely. Even when reapportionment led to new maps, most legislators were more concerned with protecting their own seats than with increasing the number of seats held by their party. As a result, some districts had gone decades without significant adjustment, even as the US population changed from largely rural to largely urban. By the early 1960s, some electoral districts had populations several times greater than those of their more rural neighbors.

However, in its one-person-one-vote decision in *Reynolds v. Simms* (1964), the Supreme Court argued that everyone's vote should count roughly the same regardless of where they lived.[11] Districts had to be adjusted so they would have roughly equal populations. Several states therefore had to make dramatic changes to their electoral maps during the next two redistricting cycles (1970–1972 and 1980–1982). Map designers, no longer certain how to protect individual party members, changed tactics to try and create safe seats so members of their party could be assured of winning by a comfortable margin. The basic rule of thumb was that designers sought to draw districts in which their preferred party had a 55 percent or better chance of winning a given district, regardless of which candidate the party nominated.

Of course, many early efforts at post-*Reynolds* gerrymandering were crude since map designers had no good way of knowing exactly where partisans lived. At best, designers might have a rough idea of voting patterns between precincts, but they lacked the ability to know voting patterns in individual blocks or neighborhoods. They also had to contend with the inherent mobility of the US population, which meant the most carefully drawn maps could be obsolete just a few years later. Designers were often forced to use crude proxies for party, such as race or the socio-economic status of a neighborhood. Some maps were so crude they were ruled unconstitutionally discriminatory by the courts.

Proponents of the gerrymandering thesis point out that the decline in the number of moderate voters began during this period of increased redistricting. But it wasn't until later, they argue, that the real effects could be seen. A second advance in redistricting, via computer-aided map making, truly transformed gerrymandering into a science. Refined computing technology, the ability to collect data about potential voters, and the use of advanced algorithms have given map makers a good deal of certainty about where to place district boundaries to best predetermine the outcomes. These factors also provided better predictions about future population shifts, making the effects of gerrymandering more stable over time. Proponents argue that this increased efficiency in map drawing has led to the disappearance of moderates in Congress.

According to political scientist Nolan McCarty, there is little evidence to support the redistricting hypothesis alone. First, he argues, the Senate has become polarized just as the House of Representatives has, but people vote for Senators on a statewide basis. There are no gerrymandered voting districts in elections for senators. Research showing that more partisan candidates first win election to the House before then running successfully for the Senate, however, helps us understand how the Senate can also become partisan.[12] Furthermore, states like Wyoming and Vermont, which have only one Representative and thus elect House members on a statewide basis as well, have consistently elected people at the far ends of the ideological spectrum.[13] Redistricting did contribute to polarization in the House of Representatives, but it took place largely in districts that had undergone significant change.[14]

Furthermore, polarization has been occurring throughout the country, but the use of increasingly polarized district design has not. While some states have seen an increase in these practices, many states were already largely dominated by a single party (such as in the Solid South) but still elected moderate representatives. Some parts of the country have remained closely divided between the two parties, making overt attempts at gerrymandering difficult. But when coupled with the sorting phenomenon discussed above, redistricting probably is contributing to polarization, if only at the margins.

Summary

A divided government makes it difficult for elected officials to achieve their policy goals. This problem has gotten worse as US political parties have become increasingly polarized over the past several decades. They are both more likely to fight with each other and more internally divided than just a few decades ago. Some possible causes include sorting and improved gerrymandering, although neither alone offers a completely satisfactory explanation. But whatever the cause, polarization is having negative short-term consequences on American politics.

Notes

1. Drew Desilver, "The Polarized Congress of Today Has Its Roots in the 1970s," 12 June 2014, http://www.pewresearch.org/fact-tank/2014/06/12/polarized-politics-in-congress-began-in-the-1970s-and-has-been-getting-worse-ever-since/ (March 16, 2016).

2. "The Tea Party and Religion," 23 February 2011, http://www.pewforum.org/2011/02/23/tea-party-and-religion/ (March 16, 2016).

3. "The Tea Party and Religion."

4. Paul Waldman, "Nearly All the GOP Candidates Bow Down to Grover Norquist," *The Washington Post*, 13 August 2015, https://www.washingtonpost.com/blogs/plum-line/wp/2015/08/13/nearly-all-the-gop-candidates-bow-down-to-grover-norquist/ (March 1, 2016).

5. Beth Fouhy, "Occupy Wall Street and Democrats Remain Wary of Each Other," *Huffington Post*, 17 November 2011.

6. Drew Desilver, "In Late Spurt of Activity, Congress Avoids 'Least Productive' Title," 29 December 2014, http://www.pewresearch.org/fact-tank/2014/12/29/in-late-spurt-of-activity-congress-avoids-least-productive-title/ (March 16, 2016).

7. "Congressional Performance," http://www.rasmussenreports.com/public_content/politics/mood_of_america/congressional_performance (March 16, 2016).

8, "Presidential Approval Ratings – Barack Obama," http://www.gallup.com/poll/116479/barack-obama-presidential-job-approval.aspx (March 16, 2016).

9. Morris Fiorina, "Americans Have Not Become More Politically Polarized," *The Washington Post*, 23 June 2014.

10. Ian Haney-Lopez, "How the GOP Became the 'White Man's Party,'" 22 December 2013, https://www.salon.com/2013/12/22/how_the_gop_became_the_white_mans_party/ (March 16, 2016).

11. *Reynolds v. Simms*, 379 U.S. 870 (1964).

12. Sean Theriault. 2013. *The Gingrich Senators: The Roots of Partisan Warfare in Congress*. New York: Oxford University Press.

13. Nolan McCarty, "Hate Our Polarized Politics? Why You Can't Blame Gerrymandering," *The Washington Post*, 26 October 2012.

14. Jamie L. Carson et al., "Redistricting and Party Polarization in the U.S. House of Representatives," *American Politics Research* 35, no. 6 (2007): 878–904.

American Politics Benefit from the Energy and Intensity of Extremism

Trevor Whitney

Trevor Whitney is a writer for the Baines Report, governed by the LBJ School of Public Affairs at the University of Texas at Austin.

The argument that America is in the stranglehold of widening, bitter political battles has become so prevalent that it is widely accepted as true.

The problem, however, is that it's not.

Senate Democrats complained that President Obama's appointments were being blocked by an "obstructionist" Republican minority- even though only 4 out of 1,560 Obama appointees have actually been denied confirmation by the Senate since the President took office.

Republicans in Congress decry the passage of the Affordable Care Act, claiming that Democrats seek to expand the government's role in healthcare- when Republicans silently did the same thing with the adoption of Medicare Part D.

A lack of partisan division is harming this country. Republicans have succeeded at expanding the welfare state and running up large deficits despite their campaign promises. Democrats remain champions of foreign adventurism despite their effort to portray themselves as the peace party.[1] The lack of substantive difference on a majority of issues is a plague upon American political culture. The fact that valid, divergent worldviews exist is being whitewashed by cries for some undefined bipartisan compromise that is held up like a religious tenant. However, these bipartisan efforts do not actually synthesize new perspectives. Instead, they reward those who would temporarily forego their own ideological beliefs in the

"America Needs More Extremists: Confronting the Myth of Political Polarization," by Trevor Whitney, The LBJ School of Public Affairs, December 6, 2013. Reprinted by permission.

hopes of receiving reciprocity at a later, undetermined date. This quid pro quo of morality is poisonous to rational, open debate. As a result, Americans have become increasingly disappointed with the political party of their choice as they say one thing and do another.

Both political parties are guilty of throwing firebomb labels at opponents— for Democrats, "anarchists" is commonly used; for Republicans, "socialist" is the insult du jour. These labels grab a lot of attention but lack actual substance. Such is life in a world of political opinions 140 characters at a time.

Ted Cruz, the abrasive junior Senator from Texas, is labeled a modern-era extremist by his opponents. His crime? He has argued ad nauseam against a tax increase (the Affordable Care Act). If this is what passes as radical and intolerable, Americans are obviously ignorant of their own history.

America has a long history of actual anarchists and socialists, and extremists of all stripes, who have forever altered our society. Extremists of their own day have spearheaded larger movements within a resistant political culture.

Lysander Spooner was an avowed 19th century anarchist. He wrote extensively about the concept of a social contract and was an outspoken voice for abolition of slavery before any party officially adopted the position. In response to expensive government postal service and what he viewed as unconstitutional interference of private commerce, Spooner founded the American Letter Mail Company. It succeeded in lowering postage rates and substantially threatened government postage service until it prompted government suppression in 1851. For his time, Spooner was a renegade— someone who openly questioned the status quo and did not follow the rules that governed the nation. Spooner was labeled an extremist by opponents, but his efforts broke the government monopoly on mail service and later improved the lives of millions of African-Americans who would officially emerge from slavery in 1865.

Eugene Debs was the most recognizable face of socialism in the United States. During World War One, Debs ran afoul of the existing political order by speaking out against the war and urging resistance to conscription. He was arrested for sedition, was stripped of his citizenship and served ten years in prison. Socialism failed to take root in America, but Debs' unabashed criticism of an administration and defiance of draft efforts paved the way for popular opposition to future wars and to conscription during the Vietnam War. Debs' case is also often used to display how unpopular speech should still be protected. During his time, Debs was labelled a "traitor to his country" by President Woodrow Wilson. All of Debs' punishment was in reaction to his words, not actions. In 1921, the Sedition Act amendments to the Espionage Act of 1917, under which Debs' had been imprisoned, were repealed. While his defiance of the draft was radical in his time, Debs' position has come to be accepted by a majority of Americans. Today the draft does not exist and is unlikely to ever be reinstated.

America does not have a problem with polarized politics. Instead, we have a problem with a lack of courage to stand against the current political environment. The extremists that we are told plague our country don't exist. America could use more extremists from all corners of the political spectrum in order to provoke honest debate about our principles and shape our nation in the 21st century.

Notes
[1] Paul, Ron. "Liberty Defined: 50 Essential Issues that Affect Our Freedom". Grand Central Publishing, 2012.

Extremism Is Difficult to Define and Difficult to Restrict Without Curtailing Freedom of Expression in General

Courtney Radsch

Courtney Radsch is an American journalist, author, and free expression advocate. She is currently the advocacy director for the Committee to Protect Journalists and author of Cyberactivism and Citizen Journalism in Egypt: Digital Dissidence and Political Change. *She has written and been interviewed extensively about digital activism and social media in the Middle East since 2006.*

"We're stepping up our efforts to discredit ISIL's propaganda, especially online," President Barack Obama told delegates at the Leaders' Summit on Countering Violent Extremism last month. The social media counter-offensive comes amid UN reports of a 70 percent increase in what it terms "foreign terrorist fighters"—citizens of U.N. member states who have left to join Islamic State and other militant groups.

Islamic State has embraced social media as a way to attract supporters around the world, in a move governments and companies have struggled to respond to. The idea of counter narratives and of removing content and closing down social media accounts believed to be linked to Islamic State has become a major international agenda item. But the focus on the group's use of social networking has opened the door to a range of politicized efforts that appear less likely to diminish Islamic State's reach than to enable countries to use countering violent extremism measures for their own domestic agenda.

Studies of Islamic State use of social media by the US government in early 2015 and the Brookings Center for Middle East Policy between September and December 2014, estimate the

---

"Why Countering Violent Extremism Measures Can Be a Threat to Press Freedom," by Courtney Radsch, Committee to Protect Journalists, October 18, 2015. Reprinted by permission.

militant group and its supporters produce between 46,000 and 90,000 posts a day. But, as a 2012 youth-focused workshop by the Organization for Security and Co-operation in Europe (OSCE) concluded, censoring content is ineffective. Such measures are akin to Whack-A-Mole, with accounts replaced as quickly as they are deleted. Supporters of the militant group have also reacted to such efforts by turning to lesser-known video upload services, hijacking trending hashtags to amplify dissemination, and even taunting YouTube administrators about the futility of their efforts, according to reports.

Despite this, some governments are seeking to hold social media firms responsible for the monitoring and removal of content. A July meeting of the U.N. Security Council Counter-Terrorism Committee called for Internet platforms to be held liable for hosting or indexing extremist content. And with the so-called right to be forgotten ruling in the EU, Internet and telecommunications intermediaries are increasingly being called on to act as editors of the Web, as CPJ's report "Balancing Act: Press Freedom at Risk as EU Struggles to Match Action with Values," found.

Intermediary liability threatens innovation and free expression by placing the burden of monitoring content on neutral third party hosts, which is why CPJ supports reforms contained in the Manila Principles on Intermediary Liability, a set of recommended best practices prepared in coalition with leading press freedom and technology policy organizations and individuals.

Last month, rights groups helped defeat a draft provision in a US Senate appropriations bill that would have obligated Internet companies and other electronic communication services to report undefined "terrorist activity," a term that, by not being defined, risks overbroad compliance.

"[Islamic State] use of social media is unprecedented so [the Obama administration] is floundering around, flailing around trying to find an appropriate response," Alberto Fernandez, vice president of the non-profit media monitoring group Middle

East Media Research Institute and former coordinator of the US Center for Strategic Counterterrorism Communications, told me.

But it's not just the Obama administration. The glorification of terrorist acts and the online recruitment of followers has come under renewed focus since the Islamic State's expansion in Syria and Iraq, and the attacks on satirical magazine Charlie Hebdo in France in January, which killed 12 people. In the past year, several governments have moved to restrict or monitor online use under the guise of counter-terrorism measures:

- In August 2014, China blocked popular messaging apps over claims that they could be used for terrorism, according to South Korean authorities.
- At a CVE working group meeting of the Global Counterterrorism Forum in Beijing in November 2014, Turkey's remarks focused on the need to remove illegal content. (Turkey, as CPJ has previously documented, uses anti-terrorism measures to block access to networks such as Twitter and charge journalists over social media posts.)
- Balkan states agreed in March to joint efforts related to "monitoring and removing Internet content that promotes terrorism and violence... as fast as possible."
- In May, the Council of Arab Information Ministers adopted a proposal by the UAE, a key partner in US counter-propaganda efforts, to limit media coverage of "extremist religious rhetoric."
- In July, Europol, the European Union's law enforcement agency, launched its Internet Referral Unit "to combat terrorist propaganda and related violent extremist activities on the Internet."

Allowing ill-defined "extremist" content to be removed without judicial oversight or due process can too easily be used by states interested in limiting independent reporting and staving off public policy debates.

Removal of Twitter accounts for instance, has been found to limit but not eliminate the scope of Islamic State social media activities, according to the Brookings study. But whether this has any impact on broader objectives, such a preventing recruitment or funding, is up for debate. The Brookings study found that removing an account makes it harder to access a group's social network, but it also has an isolation effect that could "increase the speed and intensity of radicalization for those who do manage to enter the network."

Such moves also remove information that journalists and intelligence agencies alike rely on. The basic role of the media is to provide information and often the events depicted in content disseminated by groups such as Islamic State or Boko Haram is newsworthy. Vaguely worded counter-terrorism laws and measures can also be easily manipulated or encourage self-censorship among journalists who are uncertain of where to draw the line.

The Global Network Initiative, an alliance of tech firms and civil society groups of which CPJ is a founding member, has noted concerns over approaches including blocking material without a court order, requiring companies to proactively notify governments of potential "terrorist" content, and pressuring these companies to change their terms of service to guarantee removal of content or accounts.

"Terrorist activity is a notion that potentially covers a broad array of speech and conduct. It also puts the burden on communications providers, who are private actors, to define what is terrorist activity and what is not," Judith Lichtenberg, the network's executive director, told me. "It is both wrong in principal and difficult in practice for companies to be given this responsibility."

Putting such subjective decisions in the hands of a corporate actor without giving them sufficient guidance, and without providing oversight or requiring transparency risks privatizing censorship and infringing on protected speech. Facebook, for example, has no clear definition of terrorism. Facebook's head of public policy for Central and Eastern Europe Gabriella Cseh, says designation is based on whether a group includes violence as a way to achieve its mission. No one can support or praise a terrorist act or organizations or post graphic content, she told me. "If they say [Islamic State] members are heroes we will remove that content and that will trigger account removal."

But would a universal definition of terrorism or another U.N. resolution really help? At an OSCE expert workshop on media freedom and anti-terrorism policies that I attended last week, the challenges of defining terrorism were heard from diplomats and members of civil society who overwhelmingly acknowledged the anti-terrorism agenda often had a deleterious effect on human rights and civil liberties.

More than half of the 221 imprisoned journalists in CPJ's 2014 prison census were jailed on anti-state charges. Reporters who try to cover the activities of state-designated terrorist groups or interview their members are at risk of being accused of helping terrorist groups—three journalists working for VICE News were detained in Turkey in September over such accusations. One of them, Mohammed Ismael Rasool, is still being held. A quick click through the CPJ website shows the impact such laws have on journalists, from the persecution of the Zone 9 bloggers in Ethiopia, to restrictive laws in Egypt.

"The 'war against terrorism' waged over the past 15 years ... has shown that restricting human rights in order to combat terrorism is a serious mistake and an ineffective measure which can even help terrorists' cause," Council of Europe Human Rights Commissioner Nils Muiznieks noted. In remarks published on the council's website in March, Muiznieks expressed concern at extrajudicial website blocking in France and surveillance proposals in Europe.

Georgia Holmer, an expert on countering violent extremism at the US Institute for Peace, told me she is concerned at the ramifications of such policies. She said, "What worries me is when we export some of these tools to countries that don't have robust democracies or robust checks and balances or reform measures in place, is we are actually doing more harm than good. What type of blank check are you writing?"

Democracy Should Be Oriented Toward Reasoned Deliberation and Consensus, Not Conflict and Extremism

Robert E. Ferrell and Joe Old

Robert E. Ferrell writes about political and cultural issues. Joe Old is a faculty member of the English department at El Paso Community College.

The prism through which to view contemporary American political discourse, and particularly the Republican and Democratic presidential primaries, is deliberative democracy, especially two aspects of it: the key Habermasian notions of communicative action theory and discourse ethics. These ideas are central to how Habermas examines the way society works and explains how it could and should work. If politics proceeds on the basis of these principles, not only the optics but the substance is remarkably different from what is currently on display in spectacular, though often disappointing, fashion, not only in Republican politics, but among Democrats, too. The comparison provides a viewer the ability to judge whether the smugness with respect to American exceptionalism, including the exercise of so-called American "democracy," is justified. But Habermas's scheme, if ever implemented, is also a way of preventing system elements from colonizing lifeworld on the basis of instrumental reason and displacing society's cultural values and norms with system's narrower and limited goals and self-interests.

"The Force of the Better Argument: Americans Can Learn Something from Jürgen Habermas and 'Deliberative Democracy,'" by Robert E. Ferrell and Joe Old, Scientific Research Publishing Inc., June 23, 2016. http://file.scirp.org/Html/1-1650681_67639.htm. Licensed under CC BY 4.0 International.

Communicative Action Theory

Habermas's critique of the Enlightenment, of course, is that it is an "unfinished project" because its chief project of modernity is an unfinished project (Habermas, 1997) . He argues generally that the notion of "reason" promised through the Enlightenment is still inherent and implicit in communication, but that what came to be conceived of as a general notion of rationality that came out of the Enlightenment was a restricted form, essentially instrumental reason, and that while valid for nature is less applicable to human affairs, and in fact in the two centuries following the Enlightenment has been used to dominate, exploit, and objectify humans. The notion that communication is inherently rational is based on what is called "universal pragmatics", sometimes "formal pragmatics". As participants in society engage in the very act of communicating with each other, the communication itself implies what Habermas refers to as "validity claims". These claims are four in number: comprehensibility, truth, truthfulness and correctness, and finally appropriateness (Holub, 1991: p. 13) . Holub explains that comprehensibility is not technically part of universal pragmatics itself. The remaining three ideas are, though, and make communication rational in the three worlds human beings inhabit in Habermas's scheme: the "external world of states of affairs and objects", an "internal world of ideas, thoughts, [and] emotions," and finally, a normative "world of intersubjectively determined norms and values" (Holub, 1991) . Just spelling these ideas out provides a minimal set of standards by which one can compare the actual utterances in the 2016 election season to what could result if the system had a more solid foundation than America's mythology about itself (specifically "American exceptionalism") and the instrumental reason that is everywhere evident in pursuing it. Such a shortcoming, we argue, could be managed if not avoided under Habermas's deliberative democracy.

Discourse Ethics

In a society operating as a deliberative democracy, people simply go about their business interacting with each other attempting to conduct the important business of their society until a difference arises about how something should be done, what the norm should be. At this point, action stops and, according to Habermas, "discourse" begins until consensus is reached, a bargain is struck, or agreement is postponed as the more tractable issues are dealt with. In Habermas's idealized view, a society free of domination and exploitation proceeds on the basis of certain principles that are markedly different from how contemporary American society carries on its political (indeed almost all) of its discourse. American public communication is saturated with what Habermas calls "strategic communication", which is everywhere in evidence, particularly in advertising and public relations. Strategic communication is a nearly perfect example of instrumental reason intended to manipulate or dominate humans. Inspired by his original work on the public sphere, The Transformation of the Public Sphere, which entailed studying how free agents meeting socially in coffee houses in the late 17th century and 18th century in England, and their salon and "table society" equivalents in France and Germany, freely discussed and criticized affairs of government, gradually developing notions of how members of society could in public critique their government and society and develop ideas about how each should operate (Habermas, 1993 [1962, German]: pp. 32-35) . From this historical study, Habermas developed "idealized" ways of conducting discourse. University of York Prof. James Gordon Finlayson, has laid out the basic rules of Habermasian discourse as they are often stated today. These are as follows:

> 1. Every subject with a competence to speak and act is allowed to take part in the discourse.
>
> 2. a) Everyone is allowed to question any assertion whatsoever.

b) Everyone is allowed to introduce any assertion whatsoever into the discourse.

c) Everyone is allowed to express his attitudes, desires, and needs.

3. No speaker may be prevented, by internal or external coercion, from exercising rights as laid down in (1) and (2) above (Finlayson, 2005: p. 43).

Under such discourse, each competent speaker or participant advances whatever argument seems justified, and the authority that allows understanding and which legitimizes such argument is only "the force of the better argument" (Habermas, 1996: p. 103; Habermas, 2001: p. 89; Habermas, 1997: p. 103; Chambers, 1995: p. 238), which is to say that "the unforced force of the better argument" is the only coercion (Habermas, 1996: p. 306): there is no intimidation by social or economic status, no shouting down, no ridicule, no pressure from those whose voices are privileged by large quantities of "dark money" now allowed by the Citizens United decision (Deceptive debating tricks, clever rhetoric, unsupported assertions or claims can all be "handled", or dealt with, under open discourse in which the above rules are followed).

Discourse Failures

In a society attempting to operate a "deliberative democracy," the goal, with participants seeking understanding in good faith, is social integration, working together to achieve specific goals. A slight digression should make this point clearer: Superficially, this sounds like what is meant by the expression "bipartisan," which both Democrats and Republicans use with an almost maddening frequency. However, the word has an opposite meaning from the perspectives of the two political parties. As it is used, it is the furthest thing from Habermasian communicative action or Habermasian discourse. Rather, the meaning seems to be that members from both parties will act together, but the subtext is always—from each speaker's perspective—"but we will do it my way". This is but one example of the many ways the results of contemporary American political discourse almost always fall short of those obtained through genuine communicative action.

But prior to the "bipartisan" game, there are strategic communication habits that the public is so used to that they routinely escape notice. We take them for granted, but they are not the communication habits of those intending understanding with each other or intending to reach consensus. Rather they are the methods of manipulation, domination, and exploitation, the very things the Frankfurt School has been struggling against from its founding in the 1920s. For a long time now, it has been a tradition of political candidates and public officials who don't want to answer questions or deal with specific issues squarely, simply not to answer them or deal with them at all, and rather to say what they want or had planned to say, whether it is responsive or not. In this way, they avoid questions that are put to them by debate moderators, members of the news media, and even members of the public. Habermas calls this "strategic" communication, and its goal is manipulative rather than communicative. It is instrumental reason, and it takes several forms. Even in the rare event when it's pointed out to such officials that an answer, or part of one, was not responsive, another similarly strategic answer is produced, often with the expression "that's my answer" added. This phenomenon is so common that it can be observed on a daily basis in media interviews, particularly with someone seeking office. Something that makes such strategic responses a bit more difficult to detect is that they are mixed in with genuine communication that inevitably does occur, and if the questioner is a partisan of the speaker, the strategic aspect is likely to be missed anyhow or not recognized as such. Such strategic communication, incidentally, should be distinguished from what we might call "normal bias," or the tendency to present our case in a way that makes our case, or ourselves, look good. Most people expect that, and owning up to it is just a part of honest communication. Almost the last thing a strategic communicator wants to do is admit that he or she is trying to manipulate you as opposed to communicate honestly with you. In strategic communication, there is no intent to reach any understanding or consensus, and the speech act engaged in is not even intended as "communicative". Rather, operating on the basis of instrumental reason, the speech acts—from both parties—are often only strategic action, intended from the outset as manipulative and exploitive. One result, of course, is they end up turning individuals into objects, which is contrary to the sincerity and appropriateness and correctness aspects of universal pragmatics.

Strategic communicators all engage in these activities routinely in their "communications", simply saying what they want to say, oblivious to whether they deal with the question posed. Similarly, they always take a "glass half-full" or "glass half-empty" approach when commenting on issues or candidates of the opposing party. It is rare indeed for a partisan to concede that the other side has a "good point," and so the positions each takes almost always line up with the party line or the party ideology, no matter how egregiously a statement may vary from the truth or the facts.

The Electoral Layer of Democracy Lends Itself to Extremist Politics, Which Threatens the Governing Layer of Democracy

Amy Gutmann and Dennis Thompson

Amy Gutmann is President of the University of Pennsylvania and a professor of political science at the same institution. Her most recent book is Identity in Democracy. *Dennis Thompson is the Alfred North Whitehead Professor of Political Philosophy at Harvard University. Gutmann and Thompson previously coauthored* Democracy and Disagreement.

Why is compromise on major issues so hard in democratic politics when no one doubts that it is necessary? We argue that a significant source of the resistance to political compromise lies in the democratic process itself. The increasing incursion of campaigning into governing in American democracy—the "permanent campaign"[1]—encourages political attitudes and arguments that make compromise more difficult. The resistance to compromise is a problem for any democracy because it stands in the way of change that nearly everyone agrees is necessary, and thereby biases the political process in favor of the status quo.

The resistance to democratic compromise is anchored in what we call an uncompromising mindset, a cluster of attitudes and arguments that encourage standing on principle and mistrusting opponents.[2] This mindset is conducive to campaigning, but not to governing. Resistance to democratic compromise can and should be kept in check by a contrary cluster of attitudes and arguments—a compromising mindset—which favors adapting one's principles and respecting opponents. It is the mindset more appropriate for governing, because it enables politicians more readily to recognize opportunities for desirable compromise. Political scientists have

---

"The Mindsets of Political Compromise," by Amy Gutmann and Dennis Thompson, University Of Pennsylvania. Reprinted by permission.

exposed the harmful consequences of misplaced campaigning, but have not connected this problem with the mindsets we analyze here and their implications for democratic compromise.[3]

The influence of campaigning is not necessarily greater than other factors that make compromises more difficult, such as increased polarization and the immense influence of money in democratic politics. But the mindset associated with campaigning deserves greater attention than it has received because, first, it reinforces all the other factors. Even sharp ideological differences, for example, would present less of an obstacle to compromise in the absence of the continual pressures of campaigning. Second, unlike the other factors, campaigning is an essential and desirable part of the democratic process. It becomes a problem only when it interferes with another equally essential part of the process—governing.[4] Third, if we want to make democracy more friendly toward compromise, we need to understand not only the partisan positions and political interests that affect compromise but also the arguments and attitudes that politicians use to resist or support it.

Our analysis shows the need to shift the balance in democratic governing more toward the compromising mindset and the promotion of political compromises it makes possible. But our defense of compromise is consistent with, and indeed requires, a vigorous and sometimes contentious politics in which citizens press strongly-held principles and mobilize in support of bold causes. Social movements, protest struggles, and electoral campaigns are among the significant sites of this kind of politics, and they play important roles in democratic politics. But all these activities would be in vain if the democratic process did not produce the public goods that citizens seek, and protect the rights that they cherish. The success of democratic politics ultimately depends on how our leaders govern—and thus significantly on their attitudes toward compromise.

[...]

The Constraints of Campaigning

If public-spirited politicians want to make a positive difference by legislating change, why don't they anticipate the compromise problem in their campaigns and educate voters about the need for accommodation? Why do even politicians who claim to favor bipartisanship campaign with an uncompromising mindset? Surely they can foresee that this stance will stiffen the opposition and set up their supporters to resist compromise when it is time to govern.

Consider a politician running for President who declares that one of his priorities is to reform health care. Among other bold initiatives, he promises a "National Health Insurance Exchange to help increase competition by insurers" (which would include the so-called public option). He states his unequivocal opposition to any law that requires everyone to buy health insurance (the individual mandate), an approach favored by his main rival in the primary. He promises that his health care reform "won't add a dime to the deficit and is paid for upfront." Although he presents himself as willing to "reach across the aisle" and look for common ground, he offers no concessions at all during the campaign.[5]

This portrait is a recognizable likeness of Barack Obama in the campaigns leading up to the election in 2008. But imagine a more compromise-inclined Obama.[6] Instead of standing firmly in favor of a public option, this Obama decides to educate the public about the need for compromise. While expressing his own positions, he also states explicitly where he is willing to make concessions and outlines the deals he is prepared to accept. He announces that he is willing to compromise with the opponents of a public option by substituting optional state experiments. Suppose also that he anticipates one of the compromises that later was offered to try to resolve the abortion controversy: he would be willing to give states permission to bar the use of federal subsidies for insurance plans that cover abortion (and require all insurers in states that do not adopt this ban to divide their subsidy money into separate accounts so that only dollars from private premiums can be used to pay for abortions).

It is instructive to consider why no candidate is likely to campaign as this hypothetical Obama does. First, candidates are less effective in mobilizing and inspiring supporters if they talk more about prudent compromises than about their steadfast commitments. Their support and ultimately their success in the campaign depend on reaffirming their uncompromising commitment to core principles, and on distinguishing their positions sharply from those of their opponents. Voters need to see the differences between the candidates as clearly as possible.

Second, signaling a willingness to compromise on specific policies before your opponents offer anything in return is obviously not a strategy designed to achieve the most you can reasonably win in the legislative negotiations to come. This is not only a strategic imperative but also a moral requirement. Candidates have a responsibility to their followers to increase the chances of achieving what they promise. Furthermore, the process of compromise itself, properly conceived, involves mutual sacrifice, which expresses a kind of reciprocity that is absent when candidates make premature concessions.

Third, the terms of complex political compromises typically cannot be predicted in advance of negotiations. Indeed, they should not be: the most successful compromises, like the TRA, often engage the parties in modifying their own views about what is acceptable in the process of crafting the compromise. Even if Obama knew in general terms that he would need to compromise some of his campaign promises in ways that would not sit well with his base, he would have been unwise even privately to try to anticipate the specific concessions that he would be willing to make in order to pass a health care reform bill. No one could have predicted the final shape of the health care reform bill, and few could have predicted some of the issues, like abortion, that would become major sticking points.

A successful campaign strategy thus requires the opposite of a compromising mindset. It favors candidates who stand firmly on their principles, and condemn their opponents' positions at every turn. Candidates may have to modify their positions to reach independents, but that is as far as they can go, and even that gesture toward the center is often suspect in the eyes of their more ardent supporters.

But to govern, elected leaders who want to get anything done have to adopt a compromising mindset. Rather than standing tenaciously on principle, they have to make concessions. Rather than mistrusting and trying to defeat their opponents at every turn, they have to respect their opponents enough to collaborate on legislation. In their acceptance speeches, many elected officials signal their intention to move to a compromising mindset by vowing to be everyone's president—or governor, senator, or representative—and declaring now to be the time for coming together.

The problem for compromise is that the campaign does not end the day after the election; in American democracy it has become in effect permanent.[7] This is one reason why so many citizens are rightly skeptical of "coming together" pronouncements. The expectations raised by the previous campaign continue to hang over the business of governing. Even when elected leaders recognize the desirability of compromise, their staunchest supporters still want to hold them to their campaign promises, and believe that they exaggerate the need for concessions. At the same time, as soon as one campaign ends, the preparations for the next one begin. Positions remain rigid and differences sharpen even further, as both sides look toward the next election. Individual egos play a role, too. Politicians who want credit for passing legislation (or credit for stopping it) may refuse to cooperate with their allies (or try to undermine their opponents) when they don't get their way.

The more that campaigning comes to dominate governing in democratic politics, the harder compromise becomes.[8] As the mindset useful for campaigning overtakes the mindset needed for governing, leaders—wherever they stand on the political spectrum—are less likely to see, let alone seize, opportunities for desirable compromise. As Obama observed during an exchange with Congressional Republicans at their retreat just ten days after the Massachusetts election: "It's very hard to have the kind of bipartisan work" we need on health care and other problems if the "whole question is structured as a talking point for running a campaign."[9]

Campaigning in an uncompromising style plays a moral as well as a practical role in democratic politics. It is a necessary element of an electoral system with competitive elections, and therefore a legitimate part of the democratic process. But by making compromise more difficult, it obstructs governing, an equally legitimate and in many ways more central part of the process. That is the internal tension in political compromise: The democratic process requires politicians both to resist compromise and to embrace it. The uncompromising mindset that characterizes campaigning cannot and should not be eliminated from democratic politics, but when it comes to dominate governing, it obstructs the search for desirable compromises. It is like an invasive species that spreads beyond its natural habitat as it roams from the campaign to the government.

The problem is most pronounced in the US, where campaigns last longer and terms of many offices are shorter. But it is not entirely absent in any democracy in which the habits of the campaign persist in the routines of government. Several studies of the "Americanization" of campaigns in Europe and other developed democracies have found that, although the character of campaigns varies according to local customs and political culture, nearly all are looking more and more like those in the US.[10] As this trend continues, many other democracies are likely to confront the challenge of keeping campaigning in its place.

[…]

Conclusion

To campaign successfully, politicians must mobilize and inspire their supporters. They have to articulate a coherent vision distinct from that of their opponents, and present their opponents as adversaries to be mistrusted and ultimately defeated. But to govern effectively, politicians must find ways to reach agreements with their opponents, including members of their own ideologically diverse parties—even some compromises that their own supporters may see as betrayals. This tension between what is required in a democracy to win power and what is required to exercise it is manifest in what we have called uncompromising and compromising mindsets. These two clusters of attitudes and arguments arise from the distinctions between the pressures of democratic campaigning and those of governing, and they frame the way politicians and the public view the opportunities for and the outcomes of compromises. The uncompromising mindset—marked by principled tenacity and mutual mistrust—is well-suited for campaigning. The compromising mindset—characterized by principled prudence and mutual respect—is more appropriate for governing. It is not that one is legitimate and the other not. Each has its place in the democratic process. But to the extent that the uncompromising dominates the compromising mindset in the process of governing, compromises that could reduce injustice or increase welfare go unrecognized and unsupported. When the uncompromising mindset overwhelms political thinking and action, it biases the democratic process in favor of the status quo.

It would be a mistake to try to specify exactly when a leader should adopt which mindset. That would be like the attempt to specify precise principles in advance for distinguishing between acceptable and unacceptable compromises, which we have shown is bound to be under-inclusive or over-inclusive, if not both. Nevertheless, it is clear enough that the democratic deck is stacked against compromise in contemporary American politics (and, increasingly, in democratic politics more generally). The uncompromising mindset has strayed well beyond its natural environment. To tame it, politicians and citizens need to better understand it and its compromising counterpart.

Understanding more clearly these different ways of framing disagreement can help overcome the obstacles to agreement and lead to more beneficial compromises. Political polarization is of course also an obstacle, but as we have suggested, it is only part of the problem. In any case, the ways in which it affects compromise can be adequately appreciated only by probing the mindsets we have analyzed here. Political moderates with an uncompromising mindset are prone to block compromise, just as conservatives and liberals with a compromising mindset can join together when necessary to support compromise, as Ronald Reagan and Tip O'Neill did in order to pass the TRA. Senators Hatch and Kennedy were not ideological moderates, but they adopted the compromising mindset in order to craft important democratic compromises.

Even politicians with the appropriate mindsets need institutional support to succeed in democratic politics. Institutional reforms are therefore an important complement to recognizing the difficulty created by the dominance of campaigning over governing for democratic compromise.[11] Useful institutional reforms, for example, would significantly decrease the political incentives of continually raising money from special interests and increase those of collaborating across partisan and other factional lines. Yet major institutional change that would make a significant difference itself requires compromise, and the leaders who would bring it about will themselves have to set their minds to it.

Political leaders and ordinary citizens alike could benefit from seeing more clearly the strengths and weaknesses of the compromising and uncompromising mindsets, and how they interact in the democratic process. The ways that the mindsets frame disagreements are sometimes latent and often unrecognized. By more fully appreciating the very different mindsets required by campaigning and by governing, leaders and citizens are more likely to recognize opportunities to craft compromises that could make better laws for all.

Notes

1. Jones 1998; Ornstein and Mann 2000; and Heclo 2000.
2. We use "mindsets" to refer to both cognitive and dispositional states, which include how people tend to conceptualize and argue about issues and how they are inclined to act on their conceptualizations. Mindsets manifest a form of

what psychologists call cognitive bias, but we do not assume that the bias in the mindsets we discuss necessarily leads to mistaken conclusions or actions. In political science, the concept that comes closest to our use of mindset is "framing," which has been defined as "the process by which people develop a particular conceptualization of an issue or reorient their thinking about an issue" (Chong and Druckman 2007; and Druckman 2010). We focus on the mindsets of political leaders more than on those of citizens. Political philosophers generally have not studied the content of mindsets because it lacks the rigor and scope of a theory. But, as we show here, mindsets have a cognitive structure: they presuppose moral values, express arguments, and imply theoretical commitments. Critical analysis of their structures could benefit from more normative attention by political philosophers as well as from more empirical investigation by political scientists.

3. Heclo 2000.

4. It is sometimes suggested that the answer to the question of whether the "campaign style of governing" is a "positive development for democracy" turns on whether one adopts a trustee or delegate theory of representation. "The trustee preserves the distinction between campaigning and governing; delegates are much less the purists, seeking throughout their service to mirror the interests and concerns of their constituents" (Jones 2000, 196-97). But the distinction cannot be so sharp. On any democratic trustee theory, leaders must take into account the effect of their decisions on the next election, and on any plausible delegate theory, leaders must have sufficient time before being held accountable to try to carry out the policies their constituents favor.

5. The quotes and comments are adapted from Obama's statements and speeches during the campaign, available at http://origin.barackobama.com/speeches/. On the dispute with Hillary Clinton about the individual mandate, see Robertson et al. 2007.

6. In private, Obama apparently indicated that, once in office, he would be inclined to compromise on health care. Alluding to the Clintons' failed effort at reform, he said he would not develop his own plan, drop it on the Capitol steps like a stone tablet, and refuse to bargain. "If Daniel Patrick Moynihan or Bill Bradley or John Chaffee came to me with the possibility of compromising," he is reported to have said, "I'm not going to tell them, 'It's my way or the highway'" (Alter 2010, 249).

7. For the factors that support the trend toward the permanent campaign, see Heclo 2000.

8. The permanent campaign damages the democratic process in other ways as well—for example, the preoccupation with fundraising and the excessive influence of contributors—but these effects have received more attention than the damage to the possibility of compromise. See Ornstein and Mann 2000, 224-30.

9. Baker and Hulse 2010.

10. Plasser and Plasser 2002, 15-106, 343-52; and Blumler and Gurevitch 2001, 380-403.

11. For examples of these reforms, see Ornstein and Mann 2000.

CHAPTER 2

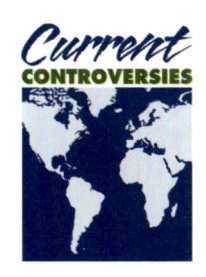

Do Political Parties Promote Extremism?

Political Parties in the United States Play a Major Role in Framing Key Political Issues and Structuring Public Opinion

Delia Baldassarri and Andrew Gelman

Delia Baldassarri is an associate professor in the department of sociology at New York University. Andrew Gelman is a professor of statistics and political science and director of the Applied Statistics Center at Columbia University.

According to theorists of political pluralism (Truman 1951; Dahl 1961; Lowi 1969; Walker 1991; see also Galston 2002; Starr 2007) as well as many scholars who have studied the structural characteristics of contemporary societies (Simmel [1908] 1955; Coser 1956; Lipset, Trow, and Coleman 1956; Lipset 1963; Lipset and Rokkan 1967; Blau 1974; Blau and Schwartz 1984), an integrated society is not a society in which conflict is absent, but rather one in which conflict expresses itself through non-encompassing interests and identities. In open societies, "segmental participation in a multiplicity of conflicts constitutes a balancing mechanism within the structure" (Coser 1956, p. 154): intrasocial conflict is sustainable as long as there are multiple and nonoverlapping lines of disagreement.

In the attempt to propose a pragmatic alternative to both the ideal of direct, popular democracy and the belief that American politics is governed by a small, unitary power elite (Mills [1956] 1970; Domhoff 1978), pluralism scholars recognize that, in practice, representative democracies do not support the ideal of equal representation. Nonetheless, these scholars maintain that a multitude of interest groups, not a close circle, have access to power. Intergroup competition, as well as institutional differentiation,

---

"Partisans without Constraint: Political Polarization and Trends in American Public Opinion," by Delia Baldassarri and Andrew Gelman, National Center for Biotechnology Information, June 13, 2014.

limits the influence of single actors, thus securing the openness of the democratic process.[1] At the same time, crosscutting interests inhibit the emergence of encompassing identities, because members' allegiance is often spread among many groups, thus diminishing the possibility of overt conflict.

Political polarization constitutes a threat to the extent that it induces alignment along multiple lines of potential conflict and organizes individuals and groups around exclusive identities, thus crystallizing interests into opposite factions. In this perspective, opinion alignment, rather than opinion radicalization, is the aspect of polarization that is more likely to have consequences on social integration and political stability. From a substantive viewpoint, if people aligned along multiple, potentially divisive issues, even if they did not take extreme positions on each of them, the end result would be a polarized society. Analytically, it can be shown that people's ideological distance and, thus, polarization depend not only on the level of radicalization of their opinions but also on the extent to which such opinions are correlated with each other—their *constraint*, in the language of Converse (1964). Nonetheless, the study of public opinion polarization has been mostly oriented to capture the radicalization of people's attitudes on single issues (looking at the variation of responses on an individual issue in the population, where more variation corresponds to more people on the extremes and fewer in the middle), while questions concerning the coherence of people's opinions across issues have generally been overlooked. In contrast, in this article we focus on the level of attitude constraint and trace time trends in issue partisanship and issue alignment in the population as a whole and within population subgroups.

According to the political pluralism model, democratic systems are characterized by crosscutting interests and identities and actual (if not equal) access to political representation for most (if not all) social groups. Results from our analysis will be used to evaluate potential deviations from this model due to *alignments of interests* that might sharpen divisions in the political arena and *group or partisan sorting* that might lead to the systematic underrepresentation (or even exclusion) of certain groups (and related interests) from the political process.[2] In so doing, we connect the debate on political polarization to broader dynamics of interest representation and political integration.

There is virtually full agreement among scholars that political parties and politicians, in recent decades, have become more ideological and more likely to take extreme positions on a broad set of political issues (McCarty, Poole, and Rosenthal 2006). Though many observers have concluded that a similar polarization process has extended to public opinion at large, scholars have shown that, over the last 40 years, American public opinion has remained stable or even become more moderate on a large set of political issues, while people have assumed more extreme positions only on some specific, hot issues, such as abortion, sexual morality, and, lately, the war in Iraq (DiMaggio, Evans, and Bryson 1996; Evans 2003; Fiorina, Abrams, and Pope 2005; Shapiro and Bloch-Elkon 2006). More systematic polarization appears in mass partisanship: those who are politically active or identify themselves with a party or ideology tend to have more extreme positions than the rest of the population. Moreover, the relation between party identification (or liberal-conservative political ideology) and voting behavior has reached its highest level in the last 50 years, after the era of partisan dealignment of the 1960s and 1970s (Bartels 2000; Hetherington 2001; Bafumi 2004).

For those scholars according to whom political polarization must imply a divergence of public opinion on a broad set of issues (DiMaggio et al. 1996) and reflect a consistent set of alternative beliefs (Fiorina et al. 2005), American public opinion is not polarized: there is evidence of attitude polarization only on a few issues, and people are often ambivalent in their preferences. Conversely, for those scholars who think that polarization is in place when broad ideological or partisan dividing lines exist, even though public opinion polarizes only on certain issues, American public opinion is polarized (Kohut et al. 2000; Green, Palmquist, and Schickler 2002; Greenberg 2004; Mayer 2004; Abramowitz and Saunders 2005; Bafumi and Shapiro 2007).

With respect to the increased partisanship of the general public, two different explanations can be advanced. One hypothesis is that citizens are changing, becoming more coherent in their political preferences over time; the other is that, even though their preferences have remained stable, citizens have responded to the growing party extremism by splitting into alternative camps.

The substantive contribution of our analysis is to offer support for the latter hypothesis by showing that Americans have become more coherent in matching their issue preferences with their party and ideology, but their level of issue constraint has remained essentially stable—and low. Thus, increased issue partisanship is not due to higher ideological coherence; rather, as suggested by Fiorina et al. (2005), it mostly arose from parties' being more polarized and therefore doing a better job at sorting individuals along ideological lines. Individuals themselves have not moved; simply, they now perceive parties as being more radical, and they split accordingly. However, party polarization might have gained momentum as party voters became more clearly divided in their preferences, thus establishing a self-reinforcing dynamic.

[…]

The Debate over Political Polarization

Political polarization is not new in American politics. According to Brady and Han's (2006, p. 120) historical analysis, "For many years, our political institutions and policy-making processes have withstood sharp divisions between the parties"; this includes the Civil War era, the turn of the 20th century, and the New Deal era. What is distinctive about the present period is the division between elite and mass polarization. There is in fact ample evidence of polarization in the party-in-government and the party-as-organization—to use the classical categories of V. O. Key (1958)—but a veil of ambiguity remains (despite a decade of research) with respect to the party in the electorate.[3]

Party and Activist Polarization

After a long period of depolarization that began at the end of World War I, political parties started to move further apart in the early 1970s. As documented by the extensive analysis of congressional roll-call voting (Poole and Rosenthal 1984, 2007; Rohde 1991; Aldrich 1996), interest groups' ratings (Poole and Rosenthal 2007, chap. 8), and other sources (Layman, Carsey, and Horowitz 2006), members of Congress have aligned at opposite ends of the liberal–conservative spectrum, and the number of moderate representatives has steadily decreased.

The electoral realignment of the southern states (Carmines and Stimson 1989; Rohde 1991; Layman et al. 2006; Ansolabehere and Snyder 2008) and the mobilization, in the middle of the 1960s, of grassroots conservative groups during the Goldwater campaign (Perlstein 2001; Brady and Han 2006) marked the beginning of a consistent movement of the Republican Party toward more conservative positions. Exiting moderate Republican members of Congress were replaced by a new cohort of socially conservative Republicans. This trend became even more prominent in the early 1990s. Simultaneously, moderate Democrats retired or were defeated, and new Democratic members were more liberal, and so the divisions between northern and southern Democrats in Congress were diminished (Wilcox 1995; Fleisher and Bond 2000; Jacobson 2005). The political issues at stake in this period well reflected the declining bipartisanship of the national elite, from Ronald Reagan's economic and social program, to the socially conservative program and confrontational strategy that characterized the Republican Party in the early 1990s, to Bill Clinton's liberal policies on matters of gay rights, abortion, taxation, and health insurance (Trubowitz and Mellow 2005).

Several scholars have identified the increased polarization of party activists as the element that has triggered party polarization. Indeed, activists have become more important in the selection of party nominees in recent decades, and they tend to have more radical views than the average citizen. In addition, the growth, starting in the 1970s, of single-issue-based interest groups has had a radicalizing effect on parties' primaries and legislative behavior in Congress (Saunders and Abramowitz 2004; Brady and Han 2006; Layman et al. 2006). Polarization shows similar trends among activists as among congressional representatives, although a clear causal relation has yet to be established. Nonetheless, once activated, party and activist polarization dynamics might have reinforced each other: the more party leaders "emphasize ideological appeals, the more likely that party will be to attract ideologically motivated activists. The involvement of these ideologically motivated activists may, in turn, reinforce ideological extremism among party leaders" (Saunders and Abramowitz 2004, p. 287). Both mechanisms of persuasion and mechanisms of selective recruitment were at work in radicalizing leaders (Fleisher and Bond 2000) and activists (Layman and Carsey 2002), with the final outcome of making the core of the Democratic Party more liberal and its Republican counterpart more conservative.

It does not come as a surprise, therefore, that after a period of decline in the importance of party identification and ideology, partisan loyalties have started to count more, to the point that, in the middle of the 1990s, their impact on voting behavior reached its highest level in at least 50 years (Abramowitz and Saunders 1998; Bartels 2000; Hetherington 2001; Bafumi 2004). Nonetheless, the fact that self-identified Republicans (or conservatives) are more likely to vote for the Republican Party today than they were 30 years ago—and the same is true of Democrats—should not be interpreted per se as a sign of public opinion polarization. Rather, "Elite polarization has clarified public perceptions of the parties' ideological differences" (Hetherington 2001, p. 619), and therefore "the public may increasingly come to develop and apply partisan predispositions" (Bartels 2000, p. 44). To what extent increased mass partisanship has brought about (or is related to) public opinion polarization—and to what extent individuals' partisanship conforms with their issue preferences—is still an open question.

Public Opinion Polarization

The debate among scholars on the level of polarization of the American public has grown along with a certain ambiguity on what opinion polarization really means and how it should be empirically measured. One way to look at public opinion polarization is to focus on the distribution of political attitudes across all Americans. If there is polarization, we should observe a change in the shape of the opinion distribution, moving from a unimodal to a flat or bimodal distribution. DiMaggio et al. (1996), looking at the population as a whole, have documented a general trend toward consensus on racial, gender, and crime issues, stability on numerous others, and evidence of polarization only on attitudes toward abortion, the poor, and, more recently, sexual morality (Evans 2003).

But one might want to track changes between subgroups of the population, distinguishing people along sociodemographic lines. For this purpose, DiMaggio et al. (1996) looked at the level of opinion disagreement between subgroups by comparing different categories of respondents. The results suggest that evidence of intergroup polarization is scarce. With respect to age, gender, education, region, and religious affiliation, the results portray stability or even instances of depolarization. Fiorina et al. (2005) and Fischer and Hout (2006) reach more or less the same conclusions. In contrast, Abramowitz and Saunders (2005) suggest that the mass public is deeply divided between red states and blue states and between churchgoers and secular voters.

Alternatively, one can look for changes in the distance between partisan subgroups, distinguishing people along ideological lines. In this case, there is clear evidence of polarization between self-identified liberals and conservatives, as well as among party affiliates and political activists (DiMaggio et al. 1996; Abramowitz and Saunders 2005; Fiorina et al. 2005). Bafumi and Shapiro (2007), analyzing the trend in the mean position of Democrats and Republicans and liberals and conservatives with respect to a large set of political issues, have found that partisans and ideologues are increasingly divided not only on issues such as abortion, gay rights, and the role of religion, but also on issues of race and civil rights. Similarly, Layman and Carsey (2002) have found that attitude constraint between social welfare and moral issues has increased among party identifiers (i.e., people who identify with a political party). Finally, looking at party voters, the divide between Democrats and Republicans has greatly increased on many issues (Jacobson 2005, 2007).

In general, scholars' analyses differ because of the social or partisan categories (class, ethnicity, religious affiliation, party identification, etc.) that are thought to be relevant for mapping social division and the dimensions around which public opinion is expected to split (polarization might be confined to people's attitudes on specific issues or instead spread across a broad set of issues). The way in which these two aspects have been combined has led different scholars to different conclusions.

When the focus is on the population as a whole or on different social groups (thus slicing the population along socioeconomic lines), scholars find evidence of polarization only on a few political attitudes. This has led them to conclude that, in general, American citizens are uncertain and ambivalent and therefore more likely to take central positions than extreme positions and to combine conservative and liberal attitudes on different issues. The same scholars have also tended to look at polarization across multiple issue domains, thus emphasizing the overall stability of public opinion. In contrast, scholars who look primarily at partisan affiliations and thus slice the population along party or ideological lines have concluded that the nation is increasingly divided. They also tend to give disproportionate attention to currently salient issues such as abortion or the war in Iraq. These scenarios do not necessarily contradict each other (Baldassarri and Bearman 2007). Indeed, both are realistic—although not complete—descriptions of contemporary America.

In this article we provide a comprehensive account of trends in issue partisanship (the relation between issues and ideology) and issue alignment (the level of constraint within and between diverse issue domains), thus disentangling the effect of party ideology from dynamics of alignment in attitude preferences. Increased issue partisanship can be thought of as a reflection of parties' differentiation and elite polarization, whereas higher levels of issue alignment would suggest that citizens are increasingly splitting along multiple lines of potential conflict. While both dynamics might have consequences on political integration—an aspect that we will discuss in the conclusion of this article—issue alignment is more likely to amplify the ideological distance between citizens and thus increase public opinion polarization, while issue partisanship might foster dynamics of unequal representation.

By separately investigating the extent to which the electorate has become more ideological and actual changes in the way in which people (or some population subgroups) combine their issue preferences, we can properly address the two most popular explanations of the changes in American public opinion. One explanation argues that elite polarization has made it easier for ordinary citizens to see the differences between parties and that therefore citizens are now better at sorting themselves between Republicans and Democrats or liberals and conservatives (Hetherington 2001; Fiorina et al. 2005; Levendusky 2004). The other argues that citizens (or subgroups of them) have themselves changed and that moral issues have lined up with economic and civil rights issues to substantially radicalize people's preferences and boost their partisanship (Layman and Carsey 2002; Abramowitz and Saunders 2005; Bafumi and Shapiro 2007). Two hypotheses follow:

> *hypothesis 1.*—*If it is parties that are moving, while people›s opinions have not changed, we expect to observe increasing issue partisanship (evidence that parties are better at sorting out their voters) but no increase in constraint in people›s political attitudes— and thus no issue alignment.*
>
> *hypothesis 2a.*—*If a real movement has occurred within the population, we expect instances of issue alignment in public opinion and thus higher levels of constraint among issues and between issue domains.*

In general, growing levels of alignment of interests might challenge the political pluralist model of crosscutting interests, but this might occur solely among the political elite (hypothesis 1) or among the larger public as well (hypothesis 2a). A second potential deviation from the political pluralism model is introduced by dynamics of group or partisan sorting, leading to the systematic underrepresentation of certain social categories. We study this second aspect by analyzing time trends within population subgroups and consider some possible variants of hypothesis 2a.

In the literature on public opinion, the theme of issue consistency and constraint has been investigated for a long time, usually with the conclusion that only a minority of very interested and informed people show real opinion constraint, while the large majority of the public is "innocent of ideology" (Converse 1964, p. 241). In the last two decades, the debate has been reframed in terms of population heterogeneity, and scholars have focused on the different heuristics people deploy in their political reasoning (Sniderman, Brody, and Tetlock 1991; Lupia, McCubbins, and Popkin 2000; Baldassarri and Schadee 2006). In both cases, results suggest that there are substantial differences across citizens with respect to their level of political sophistication and that only a small group of them fully deploy ideological categories. Since politically sophisticated and active citizens are more likely to be politically influential (Katz and Lazarsfeld 1955) but also have more extreme political views (Baldassarri 2008), it is relevant to investigate whether trends in issue partisanship and alignment among the subset of politically committed citizens differ from trends in the entire population. In fact, an influential minority can affect, in the long term, the political preferences of the rest of the electorate (Layman and Carsey 2002). We therefore consider the following hypotheses:

hypothesis 2b.—*A real movement has occurred within the subset of the population that is politically more sophisticated or active.*

Within a broad set of social categories (gender, age, ethnicity, class, geographic location, etc.) some social groups are, or have the potential to become, politically influential (through lobbying and interest groups) and thus have an impact on the policy-making process—for instance, by setting the agenda. If instances of polarization occur within such groups, this might reverberate with the political elite, if not with the mass public. Present-day lines of potential social division seem to be based on economic status—often measured through education or income (Frank 2004; Ansolabehere, Rodden, and Snyder 2006*b*; Bartels 2006; Fischer and Hout 2006; McCarty et al. 2006;)—and cultural values, captured here by region and religion (Abramowitz and Saunders 2005; McVeigh and Soboleski 2007). We therefore study the differences between trends in partisanship and issue alignment for different population subgroups.

hypothesis 2c.—A real movement has occurred within some population subgroups (such as more educated and wealthier people, southerners, or churchgoers).

Many studies have documented the increased ideological consistency of party voters (e.g., Abramowitz and Saunders 1998) as well as the growing division between Republicans and Democrats on a broad range of political issues (Bafumi and Shapiro 2007; Jacobson 2007). The sorting of Republicans and Democrats along ideological lines might have translated into greater issue alignment among partisans (Layman and Carsey 2002). Given that the political elite has a vital interest in maintaining its constituency, the consolidation of voters' preferences might have an impact on parties' conduct, even if similar patterns are not visible in the population at large. This leads us to our final variation on hypothesis 2a:

hypothesis 2d.—Issue alignment has occurred among party identifiers.

Correlation as Polarization

> *The pundits like to slice-and-dice our country into red states and blue states: red states for Republicans, blue states for Democrats. But I've got news for them, too. We worship an awesome God in the blue states, and we don't like federal agents poking around in our libraries in the red states. We coach Little League in the blue states and, yes, we've got some gay friends in the red states. There are patriots who opposed the war in Iraq, and patriots who supported the war in Iraq. (Barack Obama, Democratic National Convention, July 27, 2004)*

The fans and the detractors of Senator Barack Obama's celebrated keynote address at the 2004 Democratic National Convention interpreted his lines as a plea for bipartisan politics and national unity. Nonetheless, few observers took it at face value, as an actual picture of the state of the country. This is unfortunate because, in this regard, he got it right.

For instance, in 2004, 40% of the respondents to the NES were self-declared Republicans (including leaners), but only 23% were both self-declared Republicans and conservative (32% if we consider only the subsample of people who answered both questions). Almost half of the Republicans did not perceive themselves as being ideologically conservative. If we also consider issue preferences, the constraint of people's political preferences looks even weaker. Only 12% of the respondents are Republican and conservative and oppose abortion (in part or completely), while 16% are Republican and conservative and do not favor affirmative action, and 13% are Republican and conservative and think that government should not support health insurance programs. Altogether, in our 2004 sample, only 6% of respondents are Republicans who think of themselves as conservatives, oppose abortion, and have conservative views on affirmative action and health policy. Fully 85% of self-declared Republicans are nonconservative or take a nonconservative stand on at least one of these three traditional issues. A similar picture emerges if we look at Democrats. In this case, of the 49% of the sample who are self-declared Democrats, only 36% call themselves liberals. Overall, almost 90% of Democrats are nonliberal or have nonliberal views on abortion, affirmative action, or health policy.

As we have noted above, empirical attempts at assessing the polarization of mass opinion have mostly focused on the distribution of single issues, while rarely looking at the correlation of people's opinions on different political issues. From a substantive point of view, it makes sense that if people align along multiple, potentially divisive issues, even if they do not take extreme positions on single issues, the end result is a polarized society. For instance, consider a population with opinions on two dimensions: color (50% of the people prefer green, 50% prefer yellow) and shape (50% prefer circle, 50% prefer triangle). If opinions are independent (thus, dimensions are orthogonal), 25% of people will prefer green circle, 25% green triangle, 25% yellow circle, and 25% yellow triangle. At the other extreme, if the two dimensions are perfectly correlated, 50% of the people will have one preference (e.g., green circle) and 50% will be in the opposite corner (yellow triangle), but the opinion distribution on the single issues will not change.

For another example, consider a population with opinions on four dimensions, following a multivariate normal distribution with mean 0 and variance 1 on each opinion and correlation r between any pair of issues. In one limiting case, the correlation between dimensions is null and the four opinions are independent; in the other limiting case, the four dimensions have correlation 1, which means that individuals hold exactly the same opinion on all four issues. In between, there are situations in which the four dimensions are correlated, with correlations of different magnitude. As the correlation between issues increases, the opinion distribution on each issue remains the same, but the ideological distance in the population increases.

To show this, we measure ideological distance in two ways. First, we compute a synthetic opinion score as the average position on the four dimensions. As the correlation increases, the variance of the average score distribution grows as well. When dimensions are positively correlated, there are more people with overall extreme views than in a context in which dimensions are not correlated, even though the opinion distribution on each single issue remains the same.

Second, we can measure polarization by returning to the concept presented at the beginning of the article of society's dividing into two homogeneous parts that are far apart from each other, and by therefore focusing on the distribution of distances between pairs of people. The more a population is polarized, the higher the variation of the distance between pairs of individuals, because they are either very close or very distant. According to our argument, we would expect that as the correlation between ideological dimensions increases, the distance between individuals that belong to the same cluster decreases, while the distance between people that belong to alternative clusters increases. Mathematically, we can divide a multivariate distribution into two pieces by finding the optimal separation that will minimize the average distances between people within each piece.[4] Here, the population is partitioned into clusters according to the sign of the opinion score previously computed. In our four-dimensional normal example, where the separate distributions on each issue remain unchanged, we find that, as correlations between issues increase, the average distance between pairs of people remains stable, the average distance between pairs of people within clusters decreases, and the average distance between pairs of people in different clusters increases.

For all these theoretical reasons, we see correlation as an important aspect of polarization that has not been captured in previous analyses of a single question at a time (or in previous analyses such as Ansolabehere, Rodden, and Snyder [2006a], which combine questions in valuable ways to get more useful and precise summaries of issue positions, but do not consider the correlations as informative in themselves). We next turn to the analysis of the correlation between political attitudes in America.

[...]

Discussion

Why are Americans so worried about political polarization? And should they be worried? Scholars and pundits seem to be concerned with polarization because of its consequences for interest representation, political integration, and social stability. Political polarization constitutes a threat to the extent that it induces alignment along multiple lines of potential conflict and organizes individuals and groups around exclusive identities, thus crystallizing the public arena into opposite factions. In contrast, intrasocial conflict is sustainable as long as there are multiple and non-overlapping lines of disagreement. Starting from these premises, we have argued that polarization has to be conceived not only as a phenomenon of opinion radicalization, but also as a process of ideological division and preference alignment.

Thinking of polarization as a process of alignment along multiple dimensions of potential conflict led us not simply to study an aspect of polarization yet to be considered, but also to address broader concerns related to its potential consequences for the political process and to ask to what extent contemporary America is moving away from the ideal of political pluralism. By distinguishing between trends in issue partisanship and issue alignment, we were able to disentangle dynamics of interest alignment that might sharpen divisions in the political arena and of group or partisan sorting that might give disproportionate voice to certain population subgroups and lead to the systematic underrepresentation of others, thus making the democratic process more unequal. In the next paragraphs, we summarize our main findings and discuss their potential consequences for political representation.

In general, we have found that people's preferences are loosely connected, and even the correlation between their preferences and partisan-ship is low. But this alone cannot be regarded as a decisive proof of the crosscutting nature of people's political interests, since such a low level of constraint is only partially interpretable as an indicator of the composite, multifaceted nature of people's political views. The scarce coherence in people's attitudes is to some extent due to their low level of political sophistication: in fact, much of the population is not interested in politics, does not follow political debate, and is minimally capable of organizing its preferences according to classical ideological categories (Converse 1964; Delli Carpini and Keeter 1996). That said, it is nonetheless informative to look at temporal and group variations in levels of issue constraint.

We first considered the trend of issue partisanship over time and concluded that the relation between people's political attitudes and their party identification or political ideology has tightened. A substantial growth in the correlation between issues and partisanship is observable for all issue domains, but the change is significantly more intense in the case of moral issues. At the beginning of the 1970s, the partisan divide was visible only for economic and, to a lesser extent, civil rights issues. Thirty years later, Democrats and Republicans (and liberals and conservatives) divided in their opinions on moral issues as well. The economic domain remains the most tightly related to party identification, followed by civil rights and moral issues, while, with respect to political ideology, moral issues are now the most distinct dividing line.

In general, our analysis adds to other scholars' findings on the increasing importance of partisanship: we show that partisanship not only has an impact on voting behavior (Bartels 2000; Hetherington 2001), but plays a more important role in partitioning voters according to their issue preferences. We confirm that moral issues have become a stable component of partisan identities, but we argue that it is by no means the only (or the most important) one. Manza and Brooks (1999) have convincingly supported the persistent importance of traditional social cleavages of class, race, and religiosity in determining voting behavior. Accordingly, our study shows that individuals have become more partisan not only on moral issues, but also on economics and civil rights.

Second, we turned to the study of issue alignment, modeling the correlation between pairs of issues, and found only feeble evidence of issue alignment. We observe a minimal increase in the correlations; moreover, the trend does not differentiate pairs of issues within and across issue domains, and it does not involve a large group of issues or a meaningful subset of them.

Taken together, these two results support our hypothesis 1, suggesting that changes in the electorate should be interpreted as an illusory adjustment of citizens to the renovated partisanship of the political elite. In other words, since the parties are now more clearly divided—and on a broader set of issues—it is easier for people to split accordingly, without changing their own views (this is why we use the term *illusory*). There has been some discussion regarding the directionality of the change, with most scholars suggesting that public opinion polarization is a consequence of elite polarization (Layman et al. 2006). Our results confirm this interpretation, since, despite partisan alignment, we found no real instances of issue alignment. If it were the case that changes in voters' preferences had affected the party elite, we would instead have found evidence of issue alignment in the electorate, since issue alignment has certainly occurred among the political elite (Poole and Rosenthal 2007). Nonetheless, as we will discuss later, the sorting of voters along party lines is likely to have had an impact on parties' strategies.

So far, we have reviewed changes in the entire population. Further examining trends in issue partisanship and alignment within population subgroups allowed us to reveal potential mechanisms of unequal representation. Population subgroups differ in their overall levels of constraint: people who are wealthier, more educated, and interested in politics show, at any moment in time, higher correlations in issue attitudes than other members of the population. More interestingly, in some cases, trends in issue partisanship and alignment also differ. Specifically, we noticed that those who are more interested in politics have grown more coherent in their beliefs on moral and civil rights issues at a faster pace than the remainder of the population, thus broadening the gap between these groups' respective levels of constraint on these issues. A similar and more striking pattern was observed among the richest third of the population, who have become more coherent in their political preferences, and in the relation between these preferences and partisanship, while the poorest have remained essentially inconsistent. We do not observe any pattern, however, when dividing the population by region or by church attendance.

Our work reinforces the findings of McCarty et al. (2006) on the relation between elite polarization and inequality by suggesting that substantial partisan and issue alignment has occurred within the resourceful and powerful group of rich Americans. The wealthier part of the political constituency knows well what it wants, and it is likely, now more than in the past, to affect the political process. This potentially increases inequality in interest representation, not only through lobbying activity and campaign financing, but also in the ballot (Bartels 2008).[5]

Finally, issue alignment has occurred among party voters, with Republicans becoming more coherent in their economic and civil rights preferences and Democrats lining up on moral issues. Party voters are more divided and therefore constitute an easily identifiable target for a party elite concerned with preserving its constituency. Since parties pay some attention to voters in defining their strategies and political agenda (Stimson 2004; McCarty et al. 2006), nonvoters, by not showing up at the polls, are undermining their representation capacity both because they do not get to choose their representatives and because parties' strategies are less likely to consider their preferences.

Finally, issue alignment has occurred among party voters, with Republicans becoming more coherent in their economic and civil rights preferences and Democrats lining up on moral issues. Party voters are more divided and therefore constitute an easily identifiable target for a party elite concerned with preserving its constituency. Since parties pay some attention to voters in defining their strategies and political agenda (Stimson 2004; McCarty et al. 2006), nonvoters, by not showing up at the polls, are undermining their representation capacity both because they do not get to choose their representatives and because parties' strategies are less likely to consider their preferences.

Moreover, it is possible that extreme positions have gained prominence within the two parties: given the partisan realignment, the average opinion within partisan subgroups is now more extreme, as documented, for instance, by Shapiro and Bafumi (2006). Party voters, having become more consistent in their political preferences, are likely to convey more extreme preferences to their party leaders. In addition, given the asymmetries in issue alignment in the two parties, it is reasonable that voters are splitting along party lines according to the issues that are most salient to them, while they do not bother to adjust their (weak) preferences on the remaining issues (Baldassarri and Bearman 2007). This, in turn, gives more leverage to the actions of single-issue advocates and interest groups, which tend to hold extreme positions (Brady and Han 2006; McCarty et al. 2006).

Voting, of course, is not the only way in which citizens can exercise their political influence. In addition, some scholars have argued that, especially in recent decades, new, individualized forms of civic participation have come to permeate large spheres of social life (Schudson 1998; Perrin 2006). Nonetheless, the rise of new participatory forms, or even new forms of citizenship—Schudson's model of "monitoring citizenship"—do not per se eliminate the impact that partisan sorting and biases in group representation might have on the political outcome. Indeed, new participatory forms, especially those requiring supervising and communicative capacity, might be affected by the same asymmetries that characterize traditional ones.

To summarize, we have found that the main change in people's attitudes has more to do with a resorting of party labels among voters than with greater constraint in their issue attitudes. This has occurred mostly because parties are more polarized and therefore better at sorting individuals along ideological lines. Such partisan realignment, although it has not induced realignment in issue preferences, does not come without consequences for the political process. In fact, party polarization may have gained momentum as party voters have become more divided. This, we believe, is the feedback mechanism that has allowed parties to continue to polarize and still win elections. In addition, increased issue partisanship, in a context in which the issue constraint of the general public is extremely low, may have had the effect of handing over greater voice to political extremists, single-issue advocates, and wealthier and more educated citizens, thus amplifying the dynamics of unequal representation.

Notes

1. As argued, e.g., by James Madison in number 10 of the *Federalist Papers* (Hamilton, Madison, and Jay [1787] 1961).

2. Like any theory of democracy, political pluralism is, first and foremost, a political philosophy. As such, it might appear ill suited to empirical analysis. Nonetheless, several aspects of the current regulatory system (e.g., norms of party and interest-group competition and division of power, as well as many social policies) are based on the principles and justified according to the logic of political pluralism, making the goal of assessing the validity of its assumptions crucial to both supporters and skeptics of this political theory.

3. For Brady and Han (2006), this disconnect is due to a lag in the nationalization of congressional elections. Polarization in presidential elections has increased, starting in the mid-1960s, while congressional elections have resisted such polarizing trends, and cross-party voting persisted through the early 1990s.

4. In statistics, this is called k-means clustering, in this case with $k = 2$; in the special case of the multivariate normal distribution, the clusters are determined by a plane slicing diagonally through the space.

5. We are not suggesting that rich people all think the same; in fact, they show great variation in their partisanship (Manza and Brooks 1999; Bafumi and Shapiro 2007; Gelman, Shor, et al. 2007; Gelman, Park, et al. 2008). We are saying that, whether Republican or Democratic, rich people have a more coherent political agenda, making them more capable of pushing through the system whatever issue they care about.

Party-Based Political Gridlock Interferes with Rational Dialogue on Key Issues

Jack Zhou

Jack Zhou is a climate researcher at Duke University's Nicholas School of the Environment.

For advocates of climate change action, communication on the issue has often meant "finding the right message" that will spur their audience to action and convince skeptics to change their minds. This is the notion that simply connecting climate change to the right issue domains or symbols will cut through the political gridlock on the issue. The difficulty then lies with finding these magic bullet messages, figuring out if they talk about climate change in the context of with national security or polar bears or passing down a clean environment to future generations.

On highly polarized issues like climate change, however, communicating across the aisle may be more difficult than simply finding the right message. Here, the worst case scenario is not simply a message failing to land and sending you back to the drawing board. Instead, any message that your audience disagrees with may polarize that audience even further in their skepticism, leaving you in a worse position than you began. As climate change has become an increasingly partisan issue in American politics, this means that convincing Republicans to reject the party line of climate skepticism may be easier said than done.

In my recent paper in Environmental Politics, I show the results from a study examining how Republican (and Republican-leaning independent) individuals react when exposed to persuasive information on climate change. I find that after these individuals are faced with messages that go against their party line on climate change, they further oppose governmental action on the

"Boomerangs versus Javelins: The Impact of Polarization on Climate Change Communication," by Jack Zhou, RealClimate, June 7, 2016. Reprinted by permission.

issue, become less willing to take personal action, and, from a psychological perspective, become even surer of their distaste for climate change.

My study asked the question: "how do Republican individuals perceive persuasive information on climate change action, and what types of information are more or less effective?" To answer this question, I conducted a survey experiment wherein respondents in the treatment conditions were asked to read a paragraph about climate change. Each paragraph linked climate change to a prominent concept in American politics (either free markets, national security, poverty alleviation, or natural disaster preparation), attributed the message to a fictional but realistic-sounding source (either a Republican former Congressman or Democrat), and ended with a call for public action on the issue. These passages were rigorously pretested to ensure realism and impact.

The experiment, conducted in March 2014, used a nationally representative sample of 478 Republicans and Republican-leaning independents, who were randomly sorted into one of the eight treatment groups or the control group, where respondents were asked in a single sentence to consider climate change as a political issue. Afterwards, all respondents were asked a series of questions to assess their support for or opposition to governmental action against climate change, their likelihood of taking personal action on the issue, and how sure they felt about their climate change opinions.

What I found was that every single treatment condition failed to convince respondents. In fact, treating Republicans with persuasive information made them more resistant to climate action regardless of the content or sourcing of that information. Overall, simply being exposed to pro-climate action communication appeared to polarize Republicans even further; they became more opposed to governmental action and less likely to take personal action compared to the control group. They also became more certain of their negative opinions on the issue, displaying significantly lower attitudinal ambivalence compared to the control group. What's more, all of these treatment effects doubled to tripled in size for respondents who reported high personal interest in politics, all statistically significant outcomes. These highly politically interested individuals make up roughly one-third of Republicans in the sample and in the United States.

These are interesting results, though perhaps not unexpected given knowledge of American climate change politics. Traditionally, political communication research has focused on a phenomenon called framing, which basically deals with how information is presented to an audience. Framing effects come in two varieties: which facets of an issue are emphasized ("message effects") and who is the communicator ("source effects"). A vast literature in political science, sociology, and psychology have shown that framing information may strongly impact how individuals perceive that information.

However, persuasive framing effects – meaning framing that shifts an individual's opinion in the direction of the frame – have been hard to come by in climate change communication research. This is likely due to the fact that the issue is very much polarized, boasting public opinion gaps in the 40 percentage point range between Democrats and Republicans on an array of different aspects of the issue. For these polarized issues, we might expect framing effects to butt up against other effects. Specifically, the theory of motivated reasoning provides an explanation of how political identity influences how individuals process information and communication.

Motivated reasoning is essentially the concept that people may be spurred to think in specific ways by forming cognitive motivations. In particular, individuals may engage in directional motivated reasoning, which means that they have a preference to believe something and will process information in order to satisfy that preference. These motivations are borne out of aspects of one's identity – those strongly held beliefs that a person understands to define him or herself. For instance, someone could be motivated by their identity as a New Yorker, an Ohio State fan, or, of course, a Democrat or a Republican. Motivations are not borne out of ignorance or irrationality or mis-education; they are oftentimes simply what makes someone that person.

In practice, motivated reasoning boils down to identity defense – motivated reasoners want to protect their beliefs. This effect manifests in two ways: a confirmation bias and a disconfirmation bias (for review, see Lodge and Taber 2013). When motivated reasoners comes across information that agrees with their prior beliefs, they tend to believe that information without a lot of conscious thought. However, when motivated reasoners are exposed to dissonant information, they tend to become critical and argue against the information. After all, simply accepting information that conflicts with their priors would weaken their sense of self. When motivations become strong enough, this process of counter-arguing can convince a motivated reasoner to be even surer of his or her preferred position and become even more polarized. This is known as a backfire or boomerang effect.

When it comes to politics, the strength of an individual's motivated reasoning is strongly tied to that person's interest in politics. This relationship makes sense for multiple reasons. Given that motivations arise from strong personal identity beliefs, political motivations go hand-in-hand with interest about the subject. Furthermore, as an individual becomes more engaged with politics, they are better able to recognize and process the political cues that align with their party and ideology. From these cues, the motivated individual can deepen their motivations. For instance, political interest helps with understanding that a pro-life stance has Republican connotations while a pro-choice position is associated with the Democratic Party. Without the relevant political savvy, these phrases lack much meaning.

In my study, I found plenty of evidence of these backfire effects when it comes to Republicans and climate change action. An example of one of these findings (support for or opposition to governmental action) is shown below to illustrate how Republicans, particularly those with high personal interest in politics, respond negatively to pro-action communication. In effect, for Republican respondents with low personal interest in politics, exposure to treatment framing seemed to have had little impact – these individuals appear generally apathetic on the issue and on politics in general. But for those with high personal interest in politics, exposure to pro-action framing triggered a considerable backfire in opposition to governmental action.

Indeed, there are many potential unseen landmines to step in when trying to persuade skeptical audiences on the issue. Say you use an ineffective message. Those frames may turn off your audience or resonate with unintended thoughts or beliefs – such as a global security message backfiring on an audience of staunch isolationists. Suppose you find an effective message but your source is seen as lacking credibility. Your audience may feel they are being pandered to and backfire that way. Even when you have an effective source and message and can produce a persuasive framing effect, there's no telling how long that effect will last before decaying or how that framing effect fares when countered with arguments from the other side that reinforce the audience's prior attitudes.

For audiences who are motivated to be skeptical about climate change, providing corrective information, such as debunking the climate pause, may not work either. Brendan Nyhan and Jason Reifler (2010) have shown that factually accurate information used to correct political misconceptions are likely to fail when they fly in the face of strongly-held prior beliefs – another backfire. Indeed, there is evidence that an individual's views on climate change are less related to education and views on science as they are to cultural and political identity (Kahan et al. 2012). Simply put, people have a tendency to believe what they want to believe.

If this is the case, what is to be done about climate change communication if Republicans are difficult to reach and the political environment on climate change remains toxic? I should preface that I do not think it is impossible to persuade Republicans to reconsider their stances on the issue. Rather, the state of polarization in American politics and on climate change in particular have stacked the deck against advocates of climate action. In addition, it is currently unclear what sorts of messages are seen as consistently persuasive, which messengers are considered credible, and if it is possible to recruit these types of messengers.

However, the issue is only growing in geopolitical import and circumstances, both political and physical, may change. Social science research suggests that framing is most effective when frames are repeatedly circulated and incorporated into political discussion, in effect shifting the societal understanding of climate change to include those frames. However, this means that, besides the times and effort needed to research effective frames and messengers, advocates need to continually reach audiences whom may be strongly resistant to such communication. This may be an inefficient use of political resources.

Instead, perhaps there are other populations who may be easier to reach, and with less gnashing of teeth. A 2014 *New York Times*/CBS News poll found that 37% of Democrats and 49% of independents thought that the impacts of climate change will not occur until sometime in the future or not at all. A 2016 Pew Research Center poll shows that just 55% of Democrats and 41% of Independents consider climate change to be an important issue for the President and Congress. These are a pool of individuals who may be, at the outset, agnostic on the issue or even in favor of action but not yet mobilized. Moreover, they are less likely to be polarized against the issue and more open to persuasive communication.

A Diverse Society Like the United States Needs More than Two Political Parties
Kristin Eberhard

Kristin Eberhard is a senior researcher at the Sightline Institute. Her research focuses on climate change, energy policy, and democratic reform.

I want a political party that represents my views. Like many Oregonians, Washingtonians, and a growing number of Americans, I'm not a Democrat, and I'm not a Republican.

Independents—people who don't identify with one of the two major parties—are the biggest and fastest-growing group of US voters. At last count, 40 percent of Americans considered themselves independent. The same is true in Cascadia: in Washington, an estimated 44 percent of registered voters identify as independent; in Oregon, one-third of registered voters are not registered Democrat or Republican. The trend is even more stark among younger Americans: nearly half of millennials consider themselves independent.

Yet Cascadians who live in the United States are continually shoe-horned into the two major parties because, like Richard Gere in *An Officer and a Gentleman*, we've got nowhere else to go.

More Parties Would Better Represent Voters' Views

The growing number of Americans who don't identify with either major party and the surprising popularity of party-outsiders Sanders and Trump indicate Americans want options outside the two major parties. Two parties can adequately represent people's views along a single axis, but when views bifurcate along two different axes, two parties cannot reflect the diversity of political views. American voters span a spectrum from progressive to

"The United States Needs More Than Two Political Parties," by Kristin Eberhard, Sightline Institute, April 28, 2016. Reprinted by permission.

conservative on a left-right cultural axis, *and* they span a spectrum from elitist* to populist on an up-down economic axis.

Using data from the Pew Research Center's 2014 Political Typology Report, I charted seven of Pew's political typologies left to right—progressive to conservative—*and* top to bottom—economic elitist to economic populist.

This two-axis analysis suggested several points:

- Culturally conservative and economically elitist Americans, the "Business Conservatives" in the upper right quadrant, feel at home in the Republican party. However, business elites are worried that rising populist sentiments may hurt their bottom line, and the elitist GOP establishment is horrified that an uncouth populist like Trump is laying claim to its party banner.
- Culturally conservative and economically populist voters, the "Steadfast Conservatives" in the lower right quadrant, are relatively satisfied with the Republican party's cultural conservatism but may feel alienated from the Republican party's elitist economic policies. It follows that many of these voters are thrilled to hear Trump trumpet a culturally conservative worldview while also expressing populist economic messages, like limiting free trade and spending taxpayer dollars solving problems at home—not playing world police. Many Trump supporters also favor increasing taxes on the wealthy.
- Culturally moderate and economically populist voters, the "Young Outsiders" and the "Hard-Pressed Skeptics" in the lower middle quadrant, are dissatisfied with both parties, possibly because both parties are too focused on cultural issues rather than economic populism. Many of these voters are delighted to hear Sanders hammer on wealth inequality, financial access to college, a living wage, limiting free trade, and solving economic problems at home rather than paying to play world police.

- Culturally progressive and economically moderate Americans—"Faith and Family Left," "Next Generation Left," and "Solid Liberals" in lower left quadrant—feel pretty happy with the Democratic party. But the Democratic establishment is uncomfortable with Sanders' strident populism.

For the parties to maintain control of their banners and for more voters to see candidates they can get excited about, the United States needs parties that represent more of this diversity of views.

Winner-Takes-All Voting Suppresses Third Parties

The United States' archaic winner-take-all voting system allows the candidate with the most votes to win the whole election, even if he or she does not win a majority of the votes. Third-party candidates are almost always doomed to fail, either to become "spoilers" who hand the election to the less popular of the two major party candidates (Nader spoiled it for Gore, Perot spoiled it for Bush) or else to get weeded out in top-two primaries like Washington's.

Bernie Sanders and Donald Trump understand the constraints of the winner-take-all system. Sanders, an Independent-Socialist-Democrat, and Trump, an Independent-Democrat-unaffiliated-Republican, figured the odds of successfully infiltrating a major party's primaries were higher than the odds of successfully running as third-party candidates. The popularity of party-outsiders Sanders and Trump shows voters are looking for views outside the two major parties' orthodoxies. But when the voting system works against third parties, third-party candidates can't win, third parties can't grow, and voters who prefer third parties can't vote their conscience without feeling like they are throwing away their votes.

Many Oregonians (including yours truly) are members of the Independent Party of Oregon: enough of us that the state awarded us major party status last year. But despite our numbers, winner-take-all voting prevents independents from winning elections in part because voters are afraid to spoil the election for their preferred Democrat or Republican candidate.

Practicality propels us to keep voting for the Democrat or the Republican. Independent voters are barred from even voting in May's closed presidential primariesunless we defect and register as Democrats or Republicans.

In most stable Western democracies, Sanders and Trump wouldn't have to foist themselves on hostile parties; they could just run on their own parties' platforms. Simple. Most Western democracies use a form of voting that enables three or four viable parties. Of the 34 OECD countries, only the United Kingdom and its former colonies Canada and the United States still use winner-take-all voting—an eighteenth-century system that enables two parties to disproportionately dominate elections. Almost all other prosperous democracies use some form of proportional representation—a twentieth-century voting systems that enable multiple parties to accurately represent voters' views.

Yet even there, the wildly unrepresentative 2015 UK election results stirred calls for adopting a more modern voting system, and Canada has vowed that 2015 will be the last first-past-the-post election it ever holds. In 1996, New Zealand broke its eighteenth-century English winner-take-all voting bondage and adopted twentieth-century proportional representation voting, immediately adding several viable parties and making the legislature represent the full range of voters.

It is time for the United States to join the civilized world and shed its archaic voting system. The Cascadian parts of the country, especially Oregon and Washington, could lead the way, as I will detail in my next article.

Proportional Representation Voting Enables Multiple Parties

Robert Reich envisions rising economic populism manifesting itself as a new "People's Party." While he is right that many people on both sides of the left-right divide are desperate for more economically populist candidates, he is, sadly, wrong that America will create a viable additional party just because lots of people really, really want one (or two).

If *really wanting* were enough, the United States would have created more viable parties during the Progressive Era. If *wanting* were enough, Ross Perot's Reform Party would still be around. The paucity of parties stems not from a lack of interest but from a lack of a modern voting system. Until the United States updates how it votes, American voters will only have two viable options on their ballots, no matter how many people click their heels and wish it weren't so.

By design, winner-take-all voting disproportionately advantages two major parties, while proportional representation voting empowers parties in proportion to how many voters their platforms actually represent.

The Example of New Zealand

New Zealand used winner-take-all voting for most of the twentieth century, and two major parties, National (conservative) and Labor (progressive), consistently won almost all the seats. Since switching to proportional representation in 1996, the Green Party (progressive, environmental), the New Zealand First Party (centrist, populist, nationalist), and the Maori Party (representing indigenous people) have gained seats in Parliament proportional to the number of voters who support them (12 percent, 9 percent, and 2 percent, respectively).

The Example of Canada

In Canada, thirteen commissions, assemblies, and reports over the years recommended proportional representation. But Canada continued to suffer disproportional elections: Stephen Harper and the Conservative Party ruled for nearly a decade even though only a plurality of voters (36 to 40 percent) voted for the Conservative Party. Conservatives formed a minority government with 36.3 percent of the votes in 2006, but won a majority 53.9 percent of the legislative seats in 2011 with just 39.6 percent of the votes.

In 2015, the Liberal Party and the progressive New Democratic Party (NDP) both campaigned on the promise to abolish first-past-the-post voting. The Liberal Party swept to power with 54.4 percent of the seats (but only 39.5 percent of the vote), while the NDP won 13 percent of the seats (with 19.7 percent of the vote). The Liberal Party favors instant runoff voting (IRV), likely because it might let Liberals continue to win close to a majority of seats. The NDP favors proportional representation (specifically, a form called Mixed Member Proportional).

Prime Minister Trudeau has promised to form a multi-party committee to explore the question of which voting system is best. The NDP recommended that, in keeping with the spirit of the exercise, committee membership should be proportional to the parties' share of the vote in fall 2015: five Liberals, three Conservatives, two New Democrats, one Bloc Quebecois, and one Green.

The US Opportunity

In the United States, hardly anyone even talks about the benefits of proportional representation. In 1967, the US Congress mandated single-member districts, foreclosing proportional representation at the federal level. Good news: there are no Constitutional barriers to repealing this law and replacing it with something like the Fair Representation Act. Bad news: passing such an act through Congress will be a hard slog. As with most important changes in the United States, national reform is a long road that starts with the states.

States can experiment and spread success. Oregon and Washington could implement proportional representation in state legislatures. As more states follow suit, a bevy of benefits would compound: more voters would gain experience electing representatives through proportional voting, viable parties would gain ground, Sanders and Trump supporters would grow accustomed to electing like-minded representatives at the state level, and Congress would feel the pressure to adopt, or at least allow, proportional voting at the national level. States could make the first inroads into reforming federal elections by creating an interstate compact for fair representation and taking it to Congress asking for permission.

Proportional Representation Could Also Boost Civic Engagement, Cripple Gerrymandering, and End Partisan Gridlock

I am not constructing an elaborate ruse to bolster my pet political party. I *am* advocating to improve democracy in Cascadia so that Cascadians can make progress towards sustainability. Updating the US voting system to one that empowers more than two major parties would not only give me, other independents, and Sanders and Trump supporters a political home; it would convey copious other benefits.

As I have previously described in greater detail, winner-take-all voting yields negative campaigns that turn off voters. Because a candidate can win by gaining more support than the other guy, but not necessarily majority support, smearing an opponent, or even sullying the whole election process so that voters simply stay home on election day, can be a successful strategy. When voters have the option to more fully express their preferences because they can rank candidates or choose a party that more closely aligns with their views, candidates and parties are motivated to attract voters to their ideas, not to repel voters from their opponents or from participating in civic life at all.

In addition to encouraging negative campaigns, winner-take-all voting also discourages voters with disproportionate or unrepresentative election results. What's the point in voting when you can never actually elect someone who represents your views? Voters who prefer third-party candidates, conservative voters who live in urban areas, and progressive voters who live in rural areas face this disheartening situation every election: if you don't agree with the plurality of voters in your district then your vote doesn't matter. Proportional representation voting encourages voters by ensuring that every vote counts. Conservatives, progressives, and third-party enthusiasts can all elect legislators in proportion to their strength at the ballot box.

A winner-take-all system also fuels the gerrymandering blight that plagues the United States. Gerrymandering can only exist when single-winner districts lines can be drawn around a particular demographic of voters. With proportional representation, it doesn't matter who draws the district lines, because districts are multi-winner or are balanced by a regional or statewide vote that ensures proportional results no matter how or by whom the districts are drawn.

Winner-take-all voting and the resulting two dominant parties also jam the system with partisan gridlock. The two-party system often rewards legislators for being obstructionist and punishes them for forming inter-party alliances to get things done. With more parties, obstructionists would become irrelevant to the art of governing, which would be carried out by skilled deal-makers. For example, imagine the United States added two additional parties—a conservative populist party that would occupy the political space around where the "Steadfast Republicans" are located in the graph above, and a moderate-progressive populist party near the "Hard-Pressed Skeptics" and "Young Outsiders." A single party could no longer shut down public functions by taking its toys and going home. The other three parties would work out solutions and ignore the obstructionists. The two populist parties and the Democrats might come together to bolster Social Security and install Universal Health Care. Or they might draw enough support from the Democrats and Republicans to ensure trade agreements include protections for the American middle class.

The Question of Governmental Effectiveness

Conventional wisdom in the United States says that, while a multi-party system might be more representative of the people, additional accuracy comes at the cost of governmental effectiveness. In a two-party system, the thinking goes, the party in charge can get things done, but in a multi-party system the small factions would be constantly fighting and never accomplish anything. If Congress is gridlocked now with two parties, just imagine what it would be like with three or four!

Researcher Arend Lijphart conducted an exhaustive international study and found that multi-party systems are *more* effective at governing, maintaining rule of law, controlling corruption, reducing violence, and managing the economy— particularly minimizing inflation and unemployment while managing the economic pressures arising from economic globalization. His conclusion boils down to: good management requires a *steady hand* more than a *strong hand*. Two-party systems provide more of the latter with a strong, decisive, government, while more representative multi-party democracies provide more of the former with steady governance.

The party in charge in a two-party system can make decisions faster, but once the other party gains control it often abruptly reverses course, throwing things into disarray. And the ruling party often has a hard time implementing decisions that they made over the vehement objections of important sectors of society, since those sectors continue to oppose the outcome at every turn. A multi-party government may take longer to form the consensus needed to make a decision, but once made, decisions are durable, implementable, and not at constant risk of being overturned.

Conclusion

A representative democracy means voters elect representatives who share their values, beliefs, and priorities. With more than one set of issues at stake, two political parties cannot possibly field candidates who reflect the different permutations of voters. The growing number of independent voters and the Sanders and Trump insurgencies demonstrate voters' discontent with the deficient representation that two major parties can offer. So while outsiders like Sanders and Trump may never win a single-winner seat like the presidency, with proportional voting, the many voters rallying to the Sanders and Trump flags could elect legislators in proportion to their numbers.

Notes

*I use the term "elitist" for lack of a better term: it represents a preference for policies that benefit the economic elite, including corporations, financial institutions, and the wealthy. Economic elitists tend to oppose policies that distribute economic benefits to working- or middle-class people, like Social Security, taxes on wealth or capital gains, limits on "free trade" to protect domestic blue-collar jobs at the expense of corporate profit, and prioritizing domestic spending that may benefit Americans broadly over international interventions that may benefit corporations.

Political Extremism Is an Ingrained Part of the American Political System

Michael Atkinson and Daniel Béland

Daniel Béland is the Canada Research Chair in Public Policy at the Johnson-Shoyama Graduate School of Public Policy at the University of Saskatchewan. Michael Atkinson is a professor at the Johnson Shoyama Graduate School of Public Policy and an associate member of the department of political studies at the University of Saskatchewan

In recent years, right-wing extremism has flourished in the United States. Last fall, for instance, the Tea Party movement encouraged the nomination of Republican midterm candidates like Sharron Angle, Rand Paul and Christine O'Donnell, whose views are well to the right of those of the median American voter. Although some of these candidates actually lost key midterm battles, the overall trend has been a radicalization of the right that makes bipartisanship hard to achieve. Earlier this year, in the House of Representatives, following the Tea Party's radical antigovernment agenda, Republicans such as Paul Ryan (Wisconsin) formulated controversial and arguably extreme proposals like the privatization of Medicare, one of the largest and most popular social programs in the United States. This summer, the debate over the federal debt ceiling saw the flourishing of radical proposals from Tea Party Republicans, including calls to dramatically reduce the size of government.

Although Fox News and other media outlets have played a major role in these developments, this extremist turn was in large part made possible by the design of American political institutions. Extremism may have its ultimate origins in the paranoid and

"American democracy and political extremism," by Michael Atkinson and Daniel Béland, Policy Options Politiques, Jennifer Ditchburn, Editor-in-Chief. October 1, 2011. Reprinted by permission.

conspiratorial dynamics of American political history, but it is American political institutions that enable the cyclical recurrence of extremism in American politics. It is not simply a matter of excessive partisanship produced by social forces and antagonistic world views. It is the amplification of these positions by an institutional architecture ill-suited to governing that has drawn increasing criticism from within the American political establishment.

Even before the Tea Party became such a central player in the political debate, close observers of the continuing American political drama had begun to despair about their political institutions. In an article describing the relative success of Germany in managing the recent recession, conservative columnist David Brooks described the United States as "an institutional weakling." On the left, in their 2005 book *Off Center*, Jacob Hacker and Paul Pierson called for institutional reforms aimed, among other things, at increasing political accountability. Far from lauding the genius of the American Constitution, there is a growing recognition that the United States faces a major institutional problem that the patriotic cult of the Constitution is increasingly unable to mask. This institutional problem, which makes current right-wing extremism so central in the first place, is America's extreme version of the separation of powers.

The separation-of-powers doctrine is praised by constitution makers around the world as the essential foundation of limited government, and Americans have taken a radical view of it. They have established a republic with a multitude of legislative forums in which credible arguments and interpretations of problems and solutions can be offered. A multiplicity of views is a good thing, but not when it immobilizes decision-making. In the 2009-10 debate over health insurance reform, a shower of legislative proposals and counterproposals contaminated one another, confused the public and provided unhelpful openings for demagogues and special interests. More recently, this summer, institutional uncertainty exacerbated the political drama over raising the federal debt ceiling, which was done just hours before the dead-line.

This unhappy spectacle of American democracy at work underscores the point that in an extreme separation-of-powers regime, there is no government and there is no opposition. The closest Americans come to a "government" is something called "the administration." The language is important. The Obama administration consists of all of those executive branch appointees, literally thousands of them, responsible for managing programs authorized and funded by Congress. As opposed to the situation prevailing in countries like Britain and Canada, for example, the president leads an appointed government, not an elected one.

It is true, of course, that political parties run the legislative affairs in both British-style parliamentary governments and the American Congress. We are used to contrasting these legislative bodies in terms of the degree of unity the parties demonstrate (that is, there is a higher level of party discipline in parliamentary systems than in the United States). But the difference is more profound than that. Consider what the parties in each legislature do once they have gained authority. In Congress, they elect their leadership; in parliamentary systems their leaders have already been elected. In Congress, the dominant party forms the majority, with one or two individuals, like former Republican senator Arlen Specter (Pennsylvania), shifting allegiances. In parliaments the dominant party or parties form the government. At the end of the process parliamentary countries have a government; the United States does not.

A similar condition applies with respect to the opposition. Because the elected president sweeps the field in a winner-take-all election, there is no constituted opposition left behind. In the case of a Democratic presidential victory like the one witnessed in November 2008, the Republican Party still exists, but its leader, the chair of the Republican National Committee, is not popularly elected and is seldom seen as a credible spokesperson. As happened after 2008 Obama's victory, thousands rush to fill the void and a handful of party leaders make a credible bid for the role, but the party that loses the presidential election has no formal constitutional responsibilities. In Congress, the senior members of the party do their best to muster a coherent message, but no one can prevent defeated vice-presidential candidates, upstart governors, self-proclaimed maverick senators or blustering talk-show hosts from claiming to speak for huge opinion blocs within the party.

This is exactly what happened after Barack Obama entered the White House in early 2009, as the Tea Party and politicians claiming to speak with a true conservative voice helped shape key political and policy debates. During the 2010 midterm primaries, Tea Party supporters successfully promoted the nomination of radical Republican congressional candidates like Rand Paul (Kentucky), who won a Senate seat at the midterm election. Although some Tea Party candidates like Sharron Angle (Nevada) and Christine O'Donnell (Delaware) lost, partly because of their extremist positions, it is undeniable that, during the two years following the election of Obama to the presidency, people like Sarah Palin filled the void on the right in the absence of a clear "opposition leader." Although the 2010 midterm elections, which led to a Republican majority in the House of Representatives, created a more institutionalized form of opposition, the true "opposition leader" will truly emerge only when the 2012 Republican presidential candidate is nominated. Meanwhile, Republican leaders in Congress, including Speaker John Boehner, must deal with the self-proclaimed, non-elected opposition of the Tea Party, which is likely to rebel if the duly constituted leadership fails to confirm extreme stances on a range of issues. The above-mentioned proposal to privatize Medicare featured in the broader but equally radical "Ryan Budget" illustrates the overt willingness of many House Republicans to make such stances on major issues in order to please their narrow electoral base, which is highly influential during the primaries. The behaviour of many Tea Party House Republicans during the 2011 debt ceiling debate provides more ground to this claim, as these actors complicated the negotiations between Democrat and Republican leaders by taking extreme stances on taxation and spending issues. For at least some House Republicans, taking such extreme conservative positions is probably the best way to secure their nomination in the 2012 Republican primaries, in which Tea Party supporters are likely to play key role.

The media are rightly being blamed for providing a platform for deliberately disruptive and meretricious commentary that has facilitated the emergence of the Tea Party. The late and unlamented program Crossfire looks embarrassingly civil when compared to the barbed broadsides that pass for journalism on Fox News. To make matters infinitely worse, the Internet has vastly increased the opportunities for falsehoods to flourish, with inspired rumours and innuendoes finding a field of voyeurs on YouTube. So the media is partly to blame for encouraging Tea Party-style extremism.

Yet the media merely amplify the polarization; it is American institutions that create the large windows of opportunity for political extremism. For instance, consider that the separation of powers makes every congressman a media target. With no authoritative voice to speak for the party and no singular government to take definitive positions, a strong element of fluidity is introduced into the policy-making process. Unlike Parliament, where a single bill is presented with the expectation that amendments will not alter its fundamental purpose, Congress sees a multitude of bills advanced with the expectation that they will be merged, gutted, abandoned or disavowed as the process unfolds. Members of Congress adjust their views in Washington based on how constituents and an organized groundswell like the Tea Party seem to be reacting to ever-changing policy proposals.

A fluid process sounds democratic. Good ideas can be tossed in from all directions, rapid adjustments made in response to public reaction, and opponents on one clause can be allies on another. But the very fact that individual lawmakers, and the administration for that matter, are free to change their minds creates a confusing "who's on first" scenario in which even close followers of the debate cannot be sure what is being considered by whom. It is in this confusion that lies and deceptions flourish. Because partisan mutual adjustment is valued in the system and practised by lawmakers on a continuing basis, claims regarding the true views of peripatetic policymakers cannot be lightly dismissed. In countries like Britain and Canada, Parliament does not operate this way. The much maligned tendency of party leaders to squelch public opposition on the part of caucus members has an upside. It is not difficult to determine a party position on any given topic, or determine that the party has no established view. And if the latter is the case, this is not an invitation for party members to float their individual trial balloons or express their personal convictions. It is an invitation to help establish in private a party position that all can defend in public.

In contrast, an extreme separation of powers privileges the mobilization of opinion blocs within civil society and allows diverse and often extreme positions a legitimacy they would be denied elsewhere. In the case of the United States, the process is vouchsafed by a commitment (more or less firm) to the acceptance of democratic outcomes and the protection of civil liberties. What this version of the separation of powers cannot deliver is accountability. Those who make accusations, including those who hold public office, and spread falsehoods are relatively immune from political disposal if they can protect a relatively narrow political base in their district and beyond. Allegations over "death panels" during the recent health care debate illustrate this sad yet institutionally embedded reality.

Within the British parliamentary system, MPs have no political base to shield them from the party's authority, with the result that citizens in parliamentary systems focus their attention on authorized political spokesmen for the dominant parties. A dramatic example of that is the political situation in Canada, where Conservative Prime Minister Stephen Harper has direct control over what his ministers and MPs say in public. In Canada, as in other parliamentary democracies, others who comment or offer advice are distinctly detached from a political process in which parties are the only ones in the bullring.

Many people believe that it is only the United States that has a separation-of-powers system, but that is incorrect. In Britain and Canada, for instance, the unity achieved by the concept of the supremacy of Parliament hides the multiple elements within Parliament that contest for power between elections. The difference is that the contest is regulated, the leadership is established and the locus of accountability is uncontested, at least in theory. None of this necessarily provides needed policy change, but there is a greater likelihood that when change comes, the opposition to it will be coherent and close to the views of the median voter. Extremism in opinion is a by-product of extremism in institutional design, as contemporary American policy and political debates attest.

This means that we cannot simply blame "American culture" or even the rise of the conservative movement for the contemporary politics of extremism in the United States. Although cultural and religious factors identified by people like Richard Hofstadter do play a role in the development of extremist opinion, it is American institutions that grant it legitimacy by deliberately fragmenting authority, and depriving the country of a coherent, institutionalized opposition. Although calls for moderation are always welcome, and potentially useful, institutional reform is the most effective way to reduce extremism in American politics. Americans do not need less partisanship, they need better partisanship. A way needs to be found to oblige parties to take greater ownership of their own agendas by insisting on adherence to party policy in exchange for the use of the party label. The dangers of conformism that such an innovation would invite pale beside the dangers of extremism that polarize the country and make good governance almost impossible.

Strong and Stable Political Parties Are Essential to the Health of American Democracy

Richard H. Pildes

Richard H. Pildes is a law professor at the New York University School of Law and a leading expert on election law. He is a member of the American Academy of Arts and Sciences and the American Law Institute, and has received recognition as a Guggenheim Fellow and a Carnegie Scholar.

For many years now I have been interested in developing more of an institutionalist and realist perspective on the dynamics of democracy and effective political power, particularly in the United States. By this I mean a focus on the systemic organization of political power and the ways that legal doctrines and frameworks, as well as institutional structures, determine the modes through which political power is effectively mobilized, organized, and encouraged or discouraged. This perspective emphasizes, among other elements, the dynamic processes through which winning coalitions are built or destroyed in the spheres of elections and governance. The mutually influential relationship between these spheres ultimately determines the ways in which our democratic institutions function or fail to function.

This focus on the organization, structure, and exercise of actual political power in elections and in governance is what, in my view, characterizes "the law of democracy"—a systematic field of study in law schools for only the last twenty years or so. To sharpen up this initial description, I would contrast the approach of the "law of democracy" to those approaches to constitutional law and theory that center on protecting and developing the dignity, or the

"Romanticizing Democracy, Political Fragmentation, and the Decline of American Government," by Richard H. Pildes, The Yale Law Journal, December 2014. Reprinted by permission.

autonomy, or the "personhood" of the individual, and ensuring the equal treatment of particularly vulnerable groups. These are the aspirations of *Taking Rights Seriously*, for example—the arresting book title that defines the approach of someone who has been much on my mind lately, my recently deceased colleague, Ronald Dworkin.

Even more, however, I want to contrast my focus on the systemic organization of political power to rights-oriented approaches applied to democracy itself. By rights-oriented approaches, I mean approaches that focus on interpreting and elaborating in normative or doctrinal terms the general, broad, political values of democracy, such as participation, deliberation, political equality, and liberty, or the associated legal rights to political association, to free speech, to the vote, or to political equality. These rights-oriented approaches typically pay less attention to the structural or systemic consequences—the effects on the organization of political power—of concretely institutionalizing these abstract ideals in specific settings. Rights-oriented perspectives also often rest, implicitly, on a conception of democracy that envisions individual citizens as the central political actors. We can see these approaches in constitutional doctrine, in reformist advocacy about democracy, and in scholarship on democracy in political theory, philosophy, and law. My suggestion, however, is that these approaches can spawn, and have spawned, doctrines and policies that undermine the capacity of the democratic system as a whole to function effectively. Instead of this rights-based orientation, I want to encourage more focus on how political power gets mobilized, gets organized, and functions (or breaks down).

In this Feature, adapted from a lecture I gave at Yale Law School in November 2013, I will illustrate this approach by addressing a problem on many of our minds, what my title calls "The Decline of American Government." In making this statement, I mean to appeal to a broad consensus of such a decline. Therefore, I do not refer specifically to an inability to act in areas of partisan conflict in which one side has a substantive policy preference for the status quo (climate change policy, for example). Rather, I refer to arenas where there is broad consensual agreement that government must act, in some fashion, but where American government now seems incapable of doing so—or where government does act, but only after bringing the country or the world to the edge of a precipice: government shutdown, the regular dancing on the knife's edge of the first US government default, and the like. I do not want to suggest that American government is in some state of extreme crisis; American democracy has faced far more dramatic challenges before, and as democratic observers from de Tocqueville to today have recognized, democracy is rarely "as bad as it looks" at any particular moment. It is enough to recognize serious dysfunction even in only particular areas to motivate a search for deeper explanations, as well as directions for possible paths forward.

Political Fragmentation

I want to offer two main ideas about how to think about the decline of America's governance capacity and effectiveness.

First, I want to suggest that we cannot understand how our democratic institutions are designed and how they function without recognizing that a uniquely American cultural sensibility and understanding of democracy—one that I view as excessively romantic, particularly in the forms it takes today—informs a good deal of the ways we design and reform our democratic institutions. This uniquely romantic conception of democracy has, I believe, perversely contributed to the decline of our formal political institutions. This will be one of my themes: the dangers of democratic romanticism.

Second, in diagnosing the causes of government's limited capacity to function effectively, there is a widespread temptation to focus on how polarized the two dominant political parties have become (as well as on whether polarization is asymmetric between the two parties). Much of the commentary on polarization has focused on the difficulty of fitting America's increasingly parliamentary-like political parties into the Constitution's institutional architecture of a separated-powers system. The understandable concern that many have today is whether in times of divided government—but not only then, given the Senate filibuster rule, which remains in place on policy matters—the absence of a "majority government" will make it too difficult to generate the kind of concerted political action required for legislation.

If the concern about polarization is best understood as one about effective governance, then we should perhaps refine the concern, particularly for pragmatists searching for potentially productive directions of plausible reforms. To do so, we should identify the issue not as political polarization alone but as one of political fragmentation. By "fragmentation," I mean the external diffusion of political power away from the political parties as a whole and the internal diffusion of power away from the party leadership to individual party members and officeholders. My claim is that, for pragmatic reformers, political fragmentation of the parties (most obviously visible, at the moment, on the Republican side, but latent on the Democratic side as well) is a more important focus of attention than polarization if we are to account for why the dynamics of partisan competition increasingly paralyze American government. The government shutdown and near financial default were not a simple product of party polarization; they reflected the inability of party leaders to bring along recalcitrant minority factions of their parties and individual members to make the deals that party leaders believed necessary. The problem is not that we have parliamentary-like parties. Rather, it might well be that our political parties are not parliamentary-like enough: party leaders are now unable to exert the kind of effective party leadership characteristic of parliamentary systems.

If this analysis is correct, stronger parties—or parties stronger in certain dimensions—ironically might be the most effective vehicle for enabling the compromises and deals necessary to enable more effective governance despite the partisan divide. I will offer a quick sketch of a few policy proposals designed to re-empower political party leaders in order to make government more functional. But the specific proposals are less important in themselves than as illustrations of a direction of reform that might enable more effective governance in the enduring context of highly polarized political parties.

Democratic Romanticism

Let me begin by impressing upon you the uniqueness of America's practices and institutions of democracy, taken as a whole, compared to those of other mature, stable democracies.

Jacksonian-era reforms have bequeathed us the world's only elected judges and prosecutors. Indeed, we elect more than 500,000 legislative and executive figures, vastly more than any other country per capita (one elected official for every 485 persons): we elect insurance commissioners, drainage commissioners, hospital boards, community college boards, local school boards, and on and on. Furthermore, we lack independent institutions to oversee the election process, such as specialized electoral courts, independent boundary-drawing commissions, and independent agencies—institutions common in most democratic countries. This leaves partisan, elected, and mostly local officials in control of much of the regulation and administration of the electoral process, out of a perverse belief that doing so makes the process more democratically accountable to "us."

Our administrative state, in general, is far more subject to democratic control than those of other well-established democratic countries. Although there have been periods in which we embraced independent administrative agencies based on ideals of political independence and expertise, such as in the Progressive and New Deal Eras, the dominant and distinct characteristic of American administrative government has been the emphasis on political control (legislative or executive) over administrative agencies or what is often called "democratic accountability." Indeed, the ever-increasing American skepticism of "expertise" and pressure for more and more "popular" or "democratic" control over our institutions makes it doubtful, in my view, that the political force could be marshaled today to create an independent central banking system, such as the Federal Reserve System created in 1913, if we were facing the issue for the first time now.

As another reflection of the degree of political control over public administration perceived to be necessary in the United States, there are roughly 1,300 positions in the federal government that require Senate confirmation, from the Supreme Court to the fifteen members of the National Council on Disability, not to mention the vast amount of time that administrators spend after appointment subject to the political pressures of myriad congressional committees before which they testify constantly. As another institutional example, our democratic culture produced an extraordinarily fragmented banking system for most of American history, from the 1830s until around the 1990s; this made American banking exceptionally unstable and prone to crises relative to the banking systems of some other democratic countries (averaging one crisis every decade).[16] Democratic understandings and politics made our banking system uniquely subject to local, popular political control; our laws generated a highly disaggregated, decentralized system of tens of thousands of "unit" banks (individual local banks, with no branches) that were regulated overwhelmingly at the state level and thus politically controlled by coalitions of local bankers and agrarian populists. Indeed, the leading political history of banking systems in different countries characterizes the American banking system throughout the 1830-1990 period as "crippled by populism."

Even more to the point for my purposes now, Progressive Era reforms, such as the state-imposed requirement that political parties choose their nominees through primary elections, have long made our political parties more subject to "popular control" than in virtually any other democracy. We take for granted both that we vote for individual candidates, rather than for political parties, and that the parties must choose their candidates in primary elections, including for the most powerful elected office in the world. But primary elections are not the norm around the world—parties and their leadership choose their standard-bearers in many democracies.

Indeed, our parties are unique in other ways that reflect our unusual understanding of popular sovereignty. Our parties have long been relatively "skeletal" organizations that do not require the regular payment of party dues, in contrast with political parties in most other countries, as well as most non-party organizations. To "join" a party in the United States is simply to check a box on a form or take a party ballot during a primary election. Patronage hiring and firing once played a role analogous to the role that membership dues in other countries play, but that, we have concluded, violates the First Amendment. In the absence of dues and the power of party leadership to choose the parties' nominees, our parties have always been less tightly structured than those in European democracies. The discipline of party control is particularly firm in countries that use closed-list proportional representation electoral systems, in which voters can vote only for parties, not individual candidates. But weakened political parties do not empower "the people"; they empower the organized interests that are most able to take advantage of a system of political parties lacking sufficient organizational strength to countervail private forces. In at least twenty-three states we bypass formal institutional politics altogether through practices of direct democracy such as ballot initiatives, referenda, and recall tools that no other democracy uses to such an extent, especially since the revival of direct democracy in America that began in 1978 with the symbol of the "property tax revolt," California's Proposition 13.

One of the best comparative accounts of the way in which the unique features of American democracy combine to affect both elections and governance remains Anthony King's book, *Running Scared: Why America's Politicians Campaign Too Much and Govern Too Little*. Using the concrete experiences of specific candidates and elected officials in the United States, Great Britain, and Canada, King identifies several features of the American democratic process that make American politicians "more vulnerable, more of the time, to the vicissitudes of electoral political politics than are the politicians of any other democratic country." The unique features that combine to create this extreme vulnerability are the extremely short terms of office in the House; the use of primary elections in addition to general elections; the weakness of American political parties, which requires American candidates to be much more dependent on their own ability to raise money and get their message out; and the high costs of campaigns in the United States compared to those in several other democratic countries.

The fact that American democracy exhibits these unique structures and features across so many different institutions in so many different domains is no accident. Underlying our institutions and practices is a singular democratic political culture that has alwaysrested on a unique vision and understanding of the ideas of "popular sovereignty" and "self-government." Indeed, I believe the very term "popular sovereignty" is invoked much more commonly in the United States than anywhere else. Put simply, I would say that American democratic culture has long had a distinctively individualistic way of understanding the "right" of self-government. This vision and the design of our political institutions have been mutually constitutive and reinforcing; as this unique understanding of popular sovereignty has led to institutional structures more subject to unusually direct popular control, the longstanding existence of these institutions has helped entrench and validate the cultural understandings. I will refer to the feature of American democratic culture embodied in the ideas and institutions that I have been describing as the "individualistic conception of democratic government."

More specifically, our culture uniquely emphasizes—I would say, romanticizes—the role and purported power of individuals and direct "participation" in the dynamics and processes of "self"-government. This culture too often envisions an individualized form of political action, in which the key democratic elements are individual citizens, often pictured in splendid isolation, and a democratic politics that arises through spontaneous generation.

This vision obscures the ways in which participation must be mobilized, organized, and aggregated to be effective; even worse, the pull of this vision often has led reformers and scholars to fail to appreciate the way in which "reforms" are likely to work in practice, given that the most effectively organized and mobilized actors will seize the advantage these reforms open up. As part of this romanticized picture of democracy, we uniquely distrust organized intermediate institutions standing between the citizen and government, such as political parties.

We can observe elements of this idealized image as far back as the Federalist Papers. Despite the brilliance and realist convictions of the Federalist Papers, these documents conceive of elections and government essentially in a kind of political vacuum. They offer no account of the critical role for intermediate political actors in mobilizing and organizing voters in elections (indeed, they conceived of elections as affairs of acclamation, not competitive political contests). Similarly, they do not provide an account of the need for organized, intermediary groups within elected government, such as caucuses and parties, to enable the concerted action necessary for government to function effectively. Like other eighteenth-century political thinkers, the Framers disdained political parties; recoiled when government soon divided into two distinct and warring Federalist and Republican camps; and viewed this division as a necessary temporary evil, not a permanent, legitimate feature of democracy. The worldview at the time of the Constitution's framing encompassed citizens, elections, and government—but not the connective tissue of political parties, caucuses, and organizations that are so essential to organizing effective political power within the spheres of elections and governance. Of course, the eighteenth century's vision of political representation was more elitist than ours, but its blindness to all of the critical intermediate organizations among citizens, elections, and government reflects a characteristically American way of thinking about democracy that has endured. We can see this in American foreign policy as well, in the naïve view that immediate elections will bestow legitimate and meaningful democracy on places emerging from non-democratic pasts, without regard to whether various underpinnings of democracy, such as a plurality of organized political groups competing for power, or a robust, independent press, have had a chance to develop.

The individualized conception of democratic government has pervasively shaped, and continues to shape, American democracy. We see this in institutional design, common critiques of democracy, and reformist efforts to "improve" American democracy. The conception is largely taken for granted, if recognized at all, let alone questioned. Since at least the Jacksonian era, the appeal to more "popular empowerment" or participation as the cure for political corruption has been a constant cultural and political theme in American democracy—even as we struggle to correct for the dysfunctions that previous generations of reform in this direction have brought about. For example, in 1974 when Congress overturned the old seniority-based congressional committee system to dilute the power of committee chairs—at the time, conservative Southern Democrats—the result was the proliferation of committees and subcommittees. Yet some have argued that by undermining the power of committee chairs and diffusing power within Congress in this more "democratic" way, the net result has been to increase the power of private interest groups to block legislation by expanding further the number of veto points in the system, thereby diluting political power.

Indeed, the central impulse behind many of our democratic reform efforts is not to criticize or challenge the individualist conception of democracy, but to insist on yet more "participation" and other ways of "empowering" individual citizens as the solution to our democratic disaffections. We require so many of our institutions to be chosen through elections, for example, on the view that "citizen" control will keep officials hewing closer to the common good, without any realistic assessment of how the electoral process actually works; with romanticized views of how much interest most citizens will take (or rather, fail to take) in voting for lower-level offices; and without regard for the degree to which organized private interests will be able to dominate in low turnout, low-salience elections. This approach is a longstanding one. For example, not only do we elect school boards in many parts of the United States, but Progressive Era policies urged that these (and other) local elections be held on a separate timetable from general elections, so that local decision making would be "more pure" and not entangled in broader political issues. Yet if turnout in school board elections is exceedingly low, it is even lower when these elections are held off-cycle; not surprisingly, the one interest that is always well represented in school board elections, no matter when they are held, is that of teachers, who have among the most direct stake in school board policies. Perhaps also not surprisingly, recent empirical work "is strikingly clear" in demonstrating that the lower the turnout in such elections, the more electoral and political influence teachers have—and the higher teacher salaries become as a result. Our culture seems to reel from one democratic dysfunction, to which the solution is more citizen empowerment, to another, in which we must face up to the perverse consequences of this prior solution, only to try yet another way to ensure more transparency and citizen control.

I want to push back a bit against that culture and the romantic vision of individualistic self-government animating it.

The Causes of Polarization

To begin to do that, I now turn to my analysis of why our political institutions have become so paralyzed in recent years.

It is well-known that our era of governance is constituted by what I have called "hyperpolarized political parties." By all conventional measures, the parties in government are more polarized than at any time since the late nineteenth century. But keep in mind that partisan polarization is not necessarily bad, or all bad, from a broader democratic perspective. Political polarization, from my point of view, is a concern primarily insofar as it affects the capacity for governance. Others might be troubled with a political culture characterized by divisiveness, lack of civil disagreement, and the like, but my dominant concern is polarization's consequences for effective governance. Indeed, polarization might well involve tragic conflicts between the domains of voting and governance, a much more general conflict in democratic practice than democratic theory has recognized. As responsible party government advocates have long argued, coherent and sharply differentiated political parties increase voter turnout, make the most salient cue in voting—the political party label—more meaningful, and through that cue enable voters to hold officeholders more meaningfully accountable. As a result, party polarization has distinct electoral benefits; it is not a matter of all cost and no benefit. We should therefore view partisan polarization as a significant problem only if and when its costs are substantial enough to outweigh these electoral benefits. Preventing government from taking effective action, even when broad agreement exists to the effect that government must act in some form, signals that the costs of polarization outweigh its benefits substantially enough to justify searching for measures that could mitigate these costs, including institutional design measures.

To understand what measures might be most effective—and to justify my argument that our search should move in a dramatically different direction than is typically suggested by those troubled by extreme partisan polarization—I need to begin by explaining the causes and suggested "cures" for our world of hyperpolarized political parties. What has caused the dramatic partisan polarization of our era? Polarization is not, in my view, a product of recent, or relatively contingent, forces or individual personalities.

I have argued that the hyperpolarization of today's parties is overwhelmingly a product of long-term historical and structural forces. These forces were launched into motion with the Civil Rights Era of the 1960s, particularly the Voting Rights Act, as African Americans (and many poor whites) began the process of becoming full political participants. It is easy to forget that, from roughly the 1890s until the Civil Rights Era, the entire South was an artificially created one-party monopoly of the Democratic Party. The process of ending this unnatural political monopoly began in 1965, but the full effects of this change did not take place overnight; it took several decades of dynamic and mutually reinforcing processes for the Democratic Party in the South to move toward the left, for a robust and fully competitive Republican Party to rise, and for conservative whites to shift their party identification for Senate, House, state, and local elections to the Republican Party.

Not until the 1990s, remarkably enough, do we see the kind of two-party political system in the South that the rest of the country had throughout the twentieth century. In my view, the racial redistricting regime of the Voting Rights Act (VRA) contributed to this process. The VRA took hold for the first time in the redistrictings of the 1990s as a result of the 1982 amendments to Section 2 of the VRA and, perhaps even more importantly, the Supreme Court's 1986 *Thornburg v. Gingles* decision. The post-1990s redistricting regime shifted the political representation of the Democratic Party in the South towards its most liberal wing, dramatically reduced the number of officeholding moderate white Democrats in the South, and facilitated the rise of many more overwhelmingly conservative and Republican districts.

Through this revolutionary set of historical changes, the two political parties, at both national and state levels, became "purified" into far more ideologically coherent entities. Voters now sort themselves into the two parties overwhelmingly, and correctly, by ideology, so that nearly all liberals are now Democrats, all conservatives now Republicans. This simply had not been the case for most of the past century.

If you accept my view on this, then it follows that the highly polarized partisan structure of our democratic politics should not be seen as aberrational. It should be understood as the "new normal." Instead of being the product of contingent features of our present institutions or our present political moment, it is the result of deep and long-term historical processes. In other words, polarization should be accepted as a fact likely to be enduring for some time, not something that we can design away.

Nonetheless, a great deal of intellectual and reformist energy has been spent on the search for reformist solutions to extreme partisan polarization. This energy has been directed to restoring "the disappearing center" in American democracy. Given the recommended remedies for polarization that I describe below, it becomes necessary to explore briefly why certain solutions for polarization are likely to be unavailing and indeed, why such "fixes" might even be perverse, if the goal is to enable a more effective set of political institutions capable of overcoming current paralysis.

"Fixes" for polarization can be categorized into two forms. The first involves changes to the institutional structures of elections that will shift the mix of candidates and officeholders to empower a critical mass of more centrist officeholders who can bridge partisan divides. These institutional-design proposals include familiar ones that have been offered—open primaries; independent commissions to perform redistricting, perhaps with instructions to maximize competition; changes to internal legislative rules—and less familiar ones: eliminating laws banning "sore-loser" candidacies; moving to instant-runoff voting; or even more radically, abolishing primaries altogether and returning to a system of candidate selection by party leaders.

On the institutional front, the two fixes that have received the most attention are ending gerrymandering and opening up primary elections to a broader electorate than just party members. These changes might be desirable for many reasons, but in determining whether institutional-design changes in these areas are likely to make a meaningful contribution to reducing partisan polarization, we ought not be too sanguine about this prospect as more empirical evidence mounts. I continue to be more optimistic that changes to the structure of primary elections could make a difference, but there is little systematic empirical evidence to support this hope.

The second category of reforms, on which I would like to focus more, seeks to reduce polarization in government by empowering "the people" more effectively. The idea is that greater citizen participation will be a solvent for political dysfunction and polarization. This idea is premised on the assumption that partisan polarization is not in us, but in our political parties; polarization in our formal politics is a corruption or distortion of the more moderate, centrist politics that we would have if only we could find ways to give "the people" more direct control or influence over elections and governance. The idea is part of a recurring wish or vision throughout American political history. But there are good reasons to distrust this idea and even to think that institutional efforts to reflect popular empowerment would make polarization worse, not better.

While earlier academic work suggested that "the public" was more centrist than those holding public office, more recent works reveal that polarization in government is not so obviously a distortion or corruption of the larger public's less polarized views. Alan Abramowitz has shown that "politically engaged citizens" are just as polarized as the parties in government. Being "engaged" in this sense means little more than taking part in the most basic forms of democratic participation, such as: voting; trying to persuade a friend or neighbor to vote; displaying a bumper sticker or yard sign; giving money; or attending a campaign rally or meeting. Abramowitz's findings therefore pose a serious challenge to the idea that more participation will translate into less polarization.

Shanto Iyengar and his co-authors have found that partisans are far more uncomfortable today than in the past with their children marrying those who identify with the other party. And while citizens overall might not be as ideologically extreme as they are partisan, we are highly sorted along partisan terms today; 92% of Republicans are more conservative than the median Democrat, while 94% of Democrats are more liberal than the median Republican (twenty years ago, the figures were 64% and 70%, respectively). The percentage of those who are consistently liberal or conservative, rather than having a mix of such views, has doubled from 10% to 21% over the past two decades. As Marc Hetherington and others report, those who identify with one party express far more negative feelings about the other party than in the past; those of the opposite party to the President now largely report not trusting the government at all. A major recent study by the Pew Research Center finds that in 1994, only 17% of Republicans and 16% of Democrats had "very unfavorable" views of the opposite party, while today 43% of Republicans and 38% of Democrats hold such views. Other social scientists suggest that the public is even more extreme in its policy views than those in office or, at the least, that those whose views are categorized as "moderate" are actually ideologically polarized too. In addition, citizens, activists, and elected officeholders now see more issues in one-dimensional, partisan terms. As Carsey and Layman find: "The data are clear: across all three major domestic issue areas—social welfare, race, and culture—there has been a steady increase in the gap between Democratic and Republican citizens, elected officials and activists." In state politics, we see a pattern similar to that in Congress. On average, state legislatures are becoming significantly more polarized.

If political engagement correlates with increased polarization, as Abramowitz documents, then we should be skeptical about whether finding ways to increase popular participation will temper polarization. In addition, participation does not sprout up spontaneously, like mushrooms after a rain. Participation has to be energized, organized, mobilized, and channeled in effective directions—all of which requires the very organizations, and the partisans, that "citizen" participation is meant to bypass. Moreover, political engagement might not just involve individuals who self-select for partisanship, but might itself be an experience that generates polarization. Furthermore, despite all the cynicism about politics today, "Americans [now] are more interested in politics, better informed about public affairs, and more politically active than at any time during the past half century." More and more of us are engaged in the ways that idealized democratic citizens are thought to be. And we are partisans. Cause and effect are difficult to disentangle here. But do you know many politically engaged people who are not partisans, outside of groups like the League of Women Voters, whose membership has dropped nearly in half since 1969, according to Putnam? Extremism in the name of moderation is no vice (that is certainly my own temperament), but it doesn't raise a lot of money or draw a lot of volunteers. We should be wary of romanticizing a more engaged public as a vehicle that will save us from hyperpolarized partisan government.

Appealing to more "participation" as a cure for polarization thus reduces to a strange kind of hope that when the politically non-engaged become more engaged, they will not behave like those who are already politically engaged. They will pass untouched through the maw of the machinery of democracy but remain the same politically uninformed innocents as when they started. But their participation will have to be mobilized, organized, directed, and at least modestly informed. Will this not make them act in the same way as citizens who are already engaged?

Let me make this point concrete by turning to the specific, crucial issue of campaign financing. I show how certain proposals that focus on empowering more citizen participation are likely to have the unintended consequence of hindering effective governance.

I will state my preference at the outset: I favor a system of public financing, but not the kind of public financing centered on individual candidates that exists in the United States (in the few places we have it). Instead, I want to suggest a system of public financing in which more of the emphasis, and more of the flow of money, is oriented toward the political parties rather than individual candidates. I will return to this proposal shortly.

But to stay on the theme of empowering greater citizen participation, some proponents of public financing have suggested that campaign financing work not through the state, as in public financing around the world, but rather through individual vouchers provided to all of us. This is a distinctively American proposal, for it reflects, I believe, the peculiar and radically individualistic culture of American democracy, along with our characteristic distrust of more organized forms of political power.

Yet it turns out that individual donors are more ideologically extreme and more polarized than non-donors—as we've just discussed, the politically engaged are more polarized than the general public. Indeed, those who donate are more ideological even than "active partisans," defined as those who identify with a political party and engage in more political activities than the mere act of voting. Even more to the point, individual campaign donors are also more ideologically extreme than most other donors as well, such as PACs and the political parties. PACs tend to focus on moderate candidates, as well as incumbents; individual donors focus on more ideologically polarized candidates. In general, groups that give for access-oriented reasons tend to finance moderates and incumbents, while ideological donors favor challengers and more extreme candidates. Put another way, the most ideologically extreme money to campaigns comes from individual donors. Moreover, recent work concludes that the voting patterns of senators most closely track the policy preferences of their individual donors, rather than those of voters in the state or even co-partisans in the state—and that this pushes senators to the ideological poles. Democratic senators are more liberal, Republicans more conservative, than their voters, but these politicians are reflective of the views of their individual donor bases.

Furthermore, candidate campaigns have become dramatically more dependent on individual donors in recent decades than on all other sources combined, such as political parties and PACs, even as our candidates and parties have become more and more polarized. In other words, as our campaign finance system has become more democratized, our politics has become more polarized. In 1990, individual contributions to campaigns provided about 25% of a campaign's money, and PACs provided about half; today, individuals are by far the largest source of direct money to campaigns (about 61% for Congress) and PAC contributions constitute less than 25%.

Here is another fact to keep in mind in seeking to understand individuals, polarization, and money: a majority of individual contributions now come from out-of-state donors. Also not surprising is that out-of-state donors are the most ideologically extreme of all contributors. Consider the kind of individuals likely to give out-of-state money to the campaigns of Elizabeth Warren and Ted Cruz, as opposed to the more moderate senators or challengers about whom most out-of-staters probably know little to nothing in the first place. Are many individual voters around the country likely to send their money to Missouri for Claire McCaskill or to Tennessee for Lamar Alexander? Democratizing campaign contributions through vouchers might well, ironically, fuel the flames of political polarization, as compared to public financing systems funded in the more traditional way, through general revenues.

Voucher proponents might believe that the polarizing effects of individual donations will disappear once "all the people" are empowered to donate through vouchers. But this neglects the collective-action dynamics that influence all political activity. People have to become both motivated and engaged enough to choose to donate and to seek out information relevant to informed donations—just as they must to vote—and informing and motivating potential donors will take political organization and mobilization. Those who are most informed and motivated are likely to be partisans, and thus the groups most equipped to take advantage of these new political openings—as with other such openings—are also likely to be more partisan.

I say all this not to pick on voucher proposals in particular but to illustrate a larger point. Unless we attend to the ways in which political power is actually mobilized, organized, exercised, and marshaled, then policy proposals based on an individualistically driven vision of politics, or on non-grounded abstract democratic ideals such as "participation" or "equality," can perversely contribute to undermining our institutional capacity to govern. If we want to adopt public financing in ways least likely to fuel partisan polarization, then more traditional forms of public financing through general revenues, rather than those based on individual donations, might be more appropriate.

[…]

Conclusion

American democracy has always rested on a balance between a mythology of "popular sovereignty" and the reality of what is needed to organize political and governing power effectively. The key to effective democracy might be cast in the following way: we need to sustain the appropriate elements of popular participation while maintaining a coherent and decisive enough structure of political leadership to enable effective governance.

We have to be careful not be seduced by an overly romantic and individualized conception of democracy that has a deeper resonance in American political culture and history than in any other nation. We should also be careful about invoking democratic values, such as political equality, freedom of association and speech, and participation, in overly idealized and abstract terms that fail to attend to the actual consequences of institutionalizing these values in particular ways on effective political power and governance. This is a particular risk for legal scholarship and advocacy, both of which tend to be based more on analysis and argument concerning values and principles than on empirical facts about the actual organization of effective political power.

I realize there will be no rousing ovation for any of this. Who cheers for centralizing more power in the political parties at a time when the parties are at their least appealing? Who cheers, worse yet, for a particularly elitist vision of the political parties, centered on empowering party leaders? People will not "go to the streets" in favor of political parties and party elites. All this runs counter to the DNA of America's democratic sensibilities.

But that is part of my purpose: to challenge those sensibilities. In the midst of the declining governing capacity of the American democratic order, we ought to focus less on "participation" as the magical solution and more on the real dynamics of how to facilitate the organization of effective political power. I have tried, today, to give you a glimpse into this alternative, institutionalist approach to democracy and legal thought.

Political Parties Guard Against the Risks of Popular Democratic Governance

Democracy Web

Democracy Web, a project of the Albert Shanker Institute, is an online resource for the study of democracy. It has had millions of users around the world since it was launched in 2009.

> "A party of order or stability, and a party of progress or reform, are both necessary elements of a healthy state of political life."
>
> —John Stuart Mill,
> On Liberty, 1859

Political parties have often been portrayed in the popular media as corrupt or incompetent and are frequently viewed as the cause of government gridlock or the failure of democratically elected governments to deal with urgent issues. Political parties may become vehicles for powerful economic interests seeking to dominate the political process for their own private interests or serve as the basis for anti-democratic ideologies, such as fascism or communism, that seek political control over the society. Such negative manifestations of political parties, however, do not negate their essential importance as representative institutions in a democracy, nor the positive impact they may have within them. Political parties are the indispensable vehicles for citizens to engage in the democratic process — no modern democracy has existed without them.

"Essential Principles," Democracy Web. http://democracyweb.org/multiparty-system-principles. Licensed under CC-BY-ND Democracy Web.

In general, political parties are formed to reflect the spectrum of the people's views, interests, and needs, from their highest ideals to their basest instincts. As the 19th-century British philosopher John Stuart Mill suggests in the quote above, political parties in electoral democracies generally act together to create a balance or compromise between opposing and differing views. Just as importantly, political parties have been the means for inspiring and mobilizing voters to support fundamental political change when it is needed. Even in today's age of dispersed social communications, idealistic citizens seeking change turn to political parties to carry it out.

More than two centuries of political history have shown that no democracy can survive without a multiparty system in which the people are free to organize themselves into rival political organizations or rival factions within political organizations. Absent the organization of free and independent political parties, power is generally exploited by narrow cliques that pursue their own interests or it is monopolized by a single party that suppresses dissent and dispenses patronage to supporters.

Democracy Is Representative

The founders of the United States, both Federalists seeking a strong national government and Anti-Federalists opposing them, had a strong aversion to democracy. To them, democracy was direct popular rule and often cited the Greek political philosopher Aristotle, who defined democracy as "rule by the passionate, ignorant, demagogue-dominated 'voice of the people' . . . [that is] sure to produce first injustice, then anarchy, and finally tyranny." What we know today as democracy is representative government. It was this form of self-governance that the founders believed would provide the best protection of liberty against tyranny and also the best means for reflecting the varied opinions and will of the people. In their view, only representative government, with its capacity for debate and deliberation, permitted the balancing of individual interests in a large political community.

The Necessity of Political Parties

Yet, many of the founders were hostile to the idea of political parties. James Madison's *Federalist Papers* essay No. 10 famously argues that the organization of "factions" (meaning parties) would pose a serious danger to the new union. But America's own early elections, in which the founders divided among Federalists and anti-Federalists, showed how necessary — and natural — political parties were as a democratic instrument for representative government. They are the means by which citizens identify themselves politically. They organize citizens around ideological and policy platforms, establish the basis for voters to choose their representatives, and collectively represent the broad and diverse interests of the people. It is only in the framework of a pluralist party system that self-governance as the founders conceived it could be carried out.

Types of Electoral Systems & Their Influence on Parties

The multiparty system has many variants, representing the history of the struggle for democracy in different countries. Political parties in democratic countries are allowed generally to develop on their own, without specific constitutional provisions or mandates defining their number or nature. But partisan patterns are strongly influenced by a country's electoral framework. In both the United States and the United Kingdom, legislative elections are mostly conducted under a "first past the post" system. The candidate with the most votes — whether a majority or a simple plurality — wins the electoral contest. Legislative contests are held in geographically defined, single-member districts. This system favors the development of a small number of large parties since minor parties have difficulty contesting multiple districts.

Under proportional representation (PR) systems, used in most other countries, legislative seats are allocated according to a party's percentage of the vote nationally, regionally, or locally (depending on the election). This means that smaller parties can gain representation without actually defeating larger parties. Because many parties take seats in the legislature, coalitions of two or more parties are often needed to obtain a majority of members in parliament to vote in favor of forming a government, although sometimes one party may dominate to get a majority on its own. There are many forms of proportional representation or PR. Some electoral systems divide the vote into regional multi-seat districts, or require parties to win a minimum percentage to gain representation, or use different formulas (some quite complicated) to convert vote percentages into seats. PR systems generally have thresholds for the percentage of votes needed for political parties to gain seats in parliament. These range from less than 1 percent in the Netherlands to 10 percent in Turkey. Obviously, more parties gain representation with lower threshold requirements.

Aside from the respective electoral frameworks that help to create them, there is no clear dividing line between two-party dominant systems like that of the United States and United Kingdom and multi-party systems. Even where two large parties dominate they must represent broad interests and sometimes have a number of shifting factions within them. Also, even in "first past the post" systems, third and fourth parties arise as alternative outlets, while in multi-party systems with proportional representation, two larger, broad-based parties routinely serve as the core or dominant parties of rival coalitions.

Platforms and Ideologies

Major political parties generally represent different ideologies, namely sets of ideas about the role of government and the organization of society. In Europe, parties can be grouped under a few general labels according to their places on the political and ideological spectrum. The terms "right" and "left" were originally used to identify the two main sides of the political spectrum in the French Revolution: those wanting to keep a constitutional monarchy were seated on the right of the assembly hall and those favoring a citizens' republic on the left. "Right" now encompasses several political groupings supporting the maintenance of the existing order of things: these include Conservatives, who defend political, economic, and social traditions and practices; Christian Democrats, who support traditional religious values and social welfare within a capitalist system; and Liberals, who are backers of free market economic principles but base their ideology on secular freedoms and not religious morals. "Left" is used to categorize several types of parties: Social Democrats and Socialists, who advocate egalitarianism and a strong state role in the economy, including ownership of property; Greens, who give priority to protecting and preserving the natural environment; and other groupings that are skeptical of business or oppose traditional social institutions or values. International organizations for each of these ideological groupings allow similar parties from different countries to exchange strategies and advice or be represented in regional or cross-regional bodies.

There are ideological movements that reject the central tenets of multiparty electoral democracy but exploit the system's freedoms and processes to seek power when there is opportunity to do so. These include fascism; Soviet and Chinese communism and their variants; and some forms of religious fundamentalism and ethnic or racial nationalism. Generally, parties with such ideologies use a utopian vision for the future to justify the imposition of a dictatorship either by violent revolution or through a coup backed by military, police, or paramilitary organizations. Other parties may sometimes be allowed to exist under their rule, but they are generally surrogates or puppet parties. Real political power is exercised solely by the governing ideological party. In these single-party systems, the ruling party is also a source of patronage, the main vehicle for personal advancement in politics and society, and a mechanism for strictly enforcing conformity to the dominant ideology. Underground parties or movements organize against such regimes, but at the risk of severe repression. Communist parties have also regularly participated in elections in democratic countries but generally have lacked large enough support to create or participate in a government. Often, these arose in support of (or as agents of) the Soviet Union, but several evolved to accept the basic democratic structure of politics in their country. Communist parties declined significantly following the collapse of communist systems in 1989–91, although in Eastern Europe "post-communist parties" were reformed and often continued to hold power.

Conclusion

The multiparty system is often criticized for the emergence of partisan conflicts and political standoffs in decision making, resulting in political gridlock. While partisan conflict and gridlock are indeed problems — it has been a recent characteristic in American democracy — the multiparty system is the fundamental and necessary bulwark of a democracy and in US history has been the means for resolving its most fundamental conflicts and crises. No other model has emerged to replace the party system. Generally, parties bring people with common interests together and provide a forum for the discussion of key issues and public policies. By joining and voting for a political party, people have the opportunity to express their support for its policy platform rather than simply endorse an individual personality. They can also peacefully express opposition to the policies of a rival party or use their vote to reject the "system" as it is currently functioning. Elections are the opportunity to give a popular mandate to leaders to implement their party's program and hold them accountable if they stray from the voters' wishes or if their initiatives fail in practice. The regular rotation of power among parties prevents the entrenchment of power and tends to curb corruption and cronyism.

Ultimately, though, the multi-party system — and democracy — relies on the respect of opposition parties for the will of the people as expressed in elections. Generally, opposition parties that obstruct the legislative or governing initiatives of majority parties tend to lose support. At the same time, democracy also relies on the understanding of ruling parties that they may soon be in the opposition. This usually keeps ruling parties from abusing the rights of their opponents so that their own rights will be protected in the event they are no longer in power.

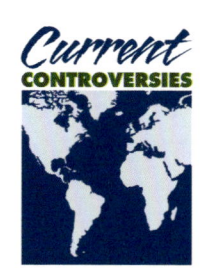

Chapter 3

Have the Dynamics of Contemporary Media Contributed to Extremism?

The Contemporary News Media Environment Raises Questions About How Networks Use Extreme Rhetoric to Attract Audiences

Alex Slack

Alex Slack was a writer for the Harvard Crimson.

More than four years ago, in February of 2000, my local CBS affiliate in Chicago tried something different. With the mantra "no water-skiing squirrels" and the expertise of veteran Chi-town anchor Carol Marin, "The 10 p.m. News with Carol Marin" attempted to take local news back in time. Gone were the menacing, sensational teasers as the station went to commercial—"What your family should know about strangulation this Christmas season"—replaced by Marin standing and reciting the day's news as impassively as a mannequin.

It was a throwback to the 1950s. And fifty years behind its time, the newscast failed. By August, there were rumblings that the CBS affiliate would can the format. By November, Carol Marin and her hardcore local news posse were toast. Their attempt at de-sensationalizing local news had only revealed the extent to which Americans (or at least Chicagoans) had become accustomed to the current sorry, sensationalized state of news in America.

Flash forward to 2004. Three 24-hour cable news channels compete for viewers. CNN captures the liberals, Fox News the conservatives and MSNBC the viewers who are transfixed by long acronyms. Fox News is winning the cable battle, and during the Republican National Convention it even beat the networks. At the same time, media intellectuals, pundits and ordinary Americans alike agree that Fox exhibits a fairly extreme bias towards the right. Eighty-nine percent of Americans trust museums for unbiased information. Thirty-six percent trust television news.

"What's Left (or Right) To Trust?" by Alex Slack, The Harvard Crimson, Inc., October 1, 2004. Reprinted by permission.

These numbers don't really add up. Americans in the twenty-first century seem to have developed a contradictory stance towards the media. On one hand, they demand their news to be exciting. On the other, they clearly wouldn't mind if their news were more trustworthy. Problem is, trustworthiness and sensationalism don't mix too well.

The lack of trust Americans have in their media is reflected by the number of media watchdog groups, each with its own left- or right-leaning agenda, that have sprung up in the last few years. There's the Media Research Center, whose mission is to "prove that liberal bias in the media does exist and undermines traditional American values." And then there's Media Matters for America, whose opposing raison d'etre is "to comprehensively monitor, analyze, and correct conservative misinformation in the US media."

There's no denying that individual media outlets cover events differently. Just look at the headlines. When interim Prime Minister of Iraq Ayad Allawi addressed a joint session of Congress recently, reporters from both Fox News and CNN attended the same speech—but they didn't write the same stories. The headline on CNN.com read, "Bush: US Won't Abandon Iraqi People." Fox News chose the simpler: "Allawi: Thank You America." Judging only from the headlines, Fox's pro-Iraq war, conservative stance comes through loud and clear. The articles also highlight different aspects of the speech, with Fox focusing on Allawi's gratefulness to America where CNN notes that the speech was made against a backdrop of growing violence and hostage-taking. There is little overlap throughout the stories. Each outlet mentions different facts, emphasizes different points and even presents the story differently (Fox News put the story at the top of its website with a picture; CNN opted for a simple hyperlinked headline). These are two different accounts of the same event. So who's telling the truth?

To answer this, we need to understand why media outlets form their own, unique biases. Research has shown that people tend to watch news from media outlets which share their own opinions. That means it's in the interest of media companies to stray from absolute neutrality. Slant the news a little, and you've instantly differentiated your newspaper or TV station from the competition. Add headlines more sensationalized and jingoistic than your competitors, and you've instantly beaten them. Wooden information-deliverers like Carol Marin don't stand a chance against the boisterous Bill O'Reilly and the seductive Paula Zahn. The media are a business, and their business is presenting biased information in a way that catches the eye of their target viewers.

It's important to keep bias and sensationalism separate. Media bias is as old as the printing press, and it's not going away. Sensationalism, however, has only as much staying power as we media consumers give it. Recently, we've been a bit too generous. When media outlets differentiate themselves by bending the truth and overstating the facts, it's tough to know what's left to trust. It's also tough to blame them for their excesses. The consumer confidence problem plaguing American media—the problem that has convinced 64 percent of America that the media are untrustworthy (up from 46 percent in mid-1989)—is not the media's fault. It's ours.

We're demanding unreasonable things from the men and women who write our news. We want the CBS ten o'clock news to be as exciting as the 9 o'clock drama. And we also want each bit of news analyzed accurately and neutrally. We want to think that the biased, sensationalized headlines flashing in front of us actually reflect the truth, even as our own demands on media make the truth harder and harder to present in a way that interests us. Until Americans stop insisting that the media cater to contradictory goals, water-skiing squirrels will carve circles around intelligent news.

Media Diversification Has Led to a New Business Model Where Sources Compete for the Loyalty of Small, Ideologically Defined Demographics

Shelley Hepworth

Shelley Hepworth, formerly a Delacorte fellow at the Columbia Journalism Review, *is now Technology Editor at the* Conversation.

After an election upset that exposed media types as out of touch with the conservative electorate, many journalists have been looking for ways to pop, or at least counter the effects, of the so-called "filter bubble." Right Richter, a media digest for people who don't usually consume right-wing news, might be a good start. As the newsletter's author, Will Sommer, writes in his first post-election edition, "We're living in the world Breitbart created now, so it's going to be more important than ever to understand what they want and what they're saying to one another."

Sommer, a 28-year-old campaign editor at *The Hill*, says he has been surprised at how little right-wing news his journalist friends who work at explicitly liberal publications read. At the same time, he acknowledges that, while there are good conservative news outlets, much of the right-wing media has become a carnival show. "For me that's great, I love it, but as far as people trying to keep up with this stuff, that complicates it," he says. Growing up in a staunchly Republican household, Sommer developed a taste for Rush Limbaugh and other conservative commentators at an early age. Even though his politics have changed, he finds himself continuing to read right-wing news just for fun. "Not everyone has the stomach for this stuff and I enjoy it, so I might as well let people know what's going on," he says.

"'We're living in the world Breitbart created now,'" by Shelley Hepworth, Columbia Journalism Review, December 9, 2016. Reprinted by permission.

Since the election, media personalities have been reaching out to their political opposites in an attempt at empathy and civilized discourse. Trevor Noah invited The Blaze commentator Tomi Lahren onto The Daily Show to discuss her extreme right-wing views. *The New York Times'* Public Editor Liz Spayd (formerly the EIC here at CJR) was a guest of Fox News's Tucker Carlson on a segment about the perceived bias of the mainstream media. CNN recently aired Van Jones's documentary *The Messy Truth*, which depicts his efforts to understand where Trump voters are coming from. The question of how to bridge the divide and what role the media should play has been a hot topic. But how did we get here?

Ken Stern, president of Palisades Media Ventures and former CEO of NPR, spent the entire week after the election consuming only conservative news, an experience he documented for *Vanity Fair*. Stern is writing a book about political polarization that aims to answer the question of why we seem to hate each other so much more now, even though data shows that we don't necessarily disagree any more than we used to. The media is partly to blame, he says. Whereas news outlets used to operate as something of a public square where people could come together to air their views, nowadays news outlets are increasingly becoming a major source of division. "I think media on all fronts are finding out that conflict really works for them," he says.

Alexander Stille, a professor at the Columbia Journalism School, traces the current bunkered state of the US media landscape back to Reagan's abolition of the Fairness Doctrine in 1987. When the doctrine was introduced in 1949, there were limited broadcast licenses. Regulators, concerned with ensuring the public was exposed to a certain plurality of views, stipulated that radio and TV license-holders had to operate in the public interest. If a TV guest advocated against smoking, the channel then had to provide an opportunity for rebuttal by, for example, someone from the smoking industry. "Broadcasting tried to do as little editorializing as possible because it was complicated and messy and their licenses might be at stake if they were seen to have lurched too far in one direction," says Stille. "That meant that broadcasting was incredibly bland and centrist."

Cable television changed that. It created the possibility of hundreds of channels, which gave rise to the idea that a plurality of viewpoints could be presented by multiple, partisan channels. Stille says that line of thought is flawed. "People don't consume news by watching five different channels. They have their channel that they tend to watch. So what we've had is that people have gotten further dug into their own news environment."

The fragmentation of the media landscape also led to the emergence of a new business model. Channels that could capture a 5 to 10 percent audience share in an inexpensive way were rewarded. Instead of having a large international news staff, outlets put talking heads on panels and amped up the conflict. "If people are shouting at each other and humiliating their guests, that makes for good political theater, and good television theater, and keeps people watching," he says. "Extreme claims capture people's attention more than bland, middle-of-the-road, on-the-one-hand, on-the-other-hand journalism." The advent of the internet only reinforced the tendency and ability for people to exist in their own personal information bubbles.

Stille links Trump and the current state of the US media to what he observed in Italy with Berlusconi. "It is to me not insignificant that the two countries where we've seen the sort of phenomenon that Trump and Berlusconi represent are two major democracies in which media was entirely deregulated," he says. "Unfortunately, the toothpaste is out of that particular tube. There's no way in the world we currently live in that somebody could reintroduce the Fairness Doctrine, as valuable as that might be."

If the entire media environment is structured in a way that produces echo chambers, then it's up to journalists to seek a way out of them at the individual level. For some, that means re-engineering their social networks; for others it means changing their media diet–all in aid of exposing themselves to a wider mix of viewpoints.

In the absence of any knowledge of, or control over, how Facebook's algorithms actually work, *Mother Jones* journalist James West (the guy who broke the story about Trump employing illegal models) decided three days after the election to friend all the Trump supporters he had interviewed on the campaign trail. "I thought, if I can simply tweak my algorithmic News Feed by adding and liking a diverse set of Trump voters, will it be true that my preferences will shift and my News Feed, and therefore worldview, will be more diverse?"

West, himself based in New York, added Trump supporters from Missouri, Pennsylvania, Ohio, Michigan, Texas, upstate New York, Virginia, Kansas, and Indiana. He's been engaging in conversations with all of them, mostly privately to start with, but already he's seeing posts they share from news outlets to which he wouldn't usually be exposed. It's giving him a clearer picture of the frustrations of Trump voters who feel they've been patronized by the mainstream press, he says.

So far, West hasn't seen any corresponding shift in the type of news articles being served to him by Facebook's algorithm, but the experiment is a work in progress, and he'll be reporting on the results for *Mother Jones*. "As an Australian, as a foreigner, it adds brushstrokes into this very detailed portrait of America that I've been trying to draw for myself over a number of years."

Not everyone agrees the exercise is worthwhile. When West posted about the experiment on Facebook, the response from *Mother Jones* readers was mixed. In the days after the election, some weren't ready to reach out to the other side, "or thought that it was a trite or even condescending idea that there was a great lot there to be understood. That in itself is sort of inherently condescending in some ways, but there were a lot of people who said, 'Yeah, this is cool, it has been a problem in my life,'" says West.

Stern, who has often found himself knee-deep in Breitbart's comments section during the course of his research, argues that simply ignoring what's being said out there isn't a useful strategy. "There [are] a lot of things I dislike about [Breitbart], intensely, but they also were early to identify issues that mattered to a group of people who felt very locked out of the political process," says Stern. "It is an important media outlet in this world now, and that means people should pay attention to it if they want to understand what's going on in our politics."

As to whether the consumption of right-wing news puts one in better touch with the electorate, Right Richter's Sommer isn't sure. Despite his understanding of the right-wing news ecosystem, he was as stunned by Trump's win as many of his lefty friends. "We were passing around an electoral map at work and I had Hillary winning like 330 or something, so obviously I don't know what I'm talking about," he jokes. But he is right that understanding the conservative media landscape has become much more important now that the president-elect is tweeting things he has read on InfoWars. "This stuff is going to be injected into the mainstream and into our consciousness much more than we've had to deal with it in the past."

The History of Fox News Illustrates How and Why the Contemporary Media Landscape Came to Embrace Ideologically Structured Coverage

David Folkenflik

David Folkenflik is an American reporter based in New York City and serving as media correspondent for National Public Radio. His work primarily appears on the NPR news programs Morning Edition **and** All Things Considered.

Tabloid blood would circulate through the arteries of what would become a new American television network, breaking the monopoly of the big three. In 1985 Rupert Murdoch acquired six television stations in the nation's largest ten markets, including New York, Los Angeles, Dallas, and Washington, D.C., from John Kluge's Metromedia conglomerate. The deal, constructed before Murdoch had acquired 20th Century Fox, put the creation of a fourth network within reach. When Murdoch bought out Marvin Davis's stake in both Fox studios and the stations that year, the Australian newspaper king was suddenly America's newest multimedia mogul—with major holdings in print, movies, and television.

At its debut in 1986, the Fox network broadcast but a night or two a week. Even when Fox became full-fledged, it provided just two hours of nightly prime-time programming. It offered magazine shows inspired more by the *New York Post* and daytime television than nightly news programs. In fact, Fox had built no indigenous news division to cover the news.

"A Current Affair" was a syndicated scandal and entertainment TV show that originated in 1986 from News Corp's flagship local TV station WNYW Channel 5 in New York City. One of its stars was Steve Dunleavy. He wore a trench coat, chain-smoked like Bogart, and cut

---

"The birth of Fox News," by David Folkenflik, Salon.com, October 19, 2013. Reprinted by permission.

a memorable figure with a jutting chin and unavoidable pompadour. And he chased just about anything with two X chromosomes. The oft-recycled claim was that he had been in coital vigor with a Scandinavian heiress late one snowy night outside a bar when a city snowplow ran over—and broke—his foot. Dunleavy was said to be so soused that he continued his aerobic affections unabated.

The tabloid columnist Pete Hamill joked, "I hope it wasn't his writing foot."

Dunleavy shone as a reporter for Murdoch's tabloid Mirror in Sydney before breaking stories for the National Star. He headed to greater glories on the Post. During the height of the scare over the Son of Sam serial killings in the New York City boroughs of Queens and Brooklyn, Dunleavy wrote a florid front-page piece advertised by the headline "Gunman Sparks Son of Sam Chase." Readers learned right before the article's conclusion that the gunman was not the Son of Sam at all.

After helping to launch "A Current Affair," Dunleavy surfaced yet again for Murdoch on the early Fox weekend show "The Reporters," another hour of gossip and crime. "In its first couple of years, television was considered a foul little business that no self-respecting journalist wanted anything to do with," Washington Post TV critic Tom Shales wrote at its debut in 1988. "Fox Broadcasting is trying to bring those days back."

"The Reporters" didn't last long, but Dunleavy never lost his luster with Murdoch. Fox did not need to develop refined taste. The early reality Fox show "Cops," an exceptionally cost-effective production that taped raids by patrolling police officers on low-level criminals, frequently beat its competition in the ratings. "The Simpsons," a spin-off of Tracey Ullman's comedy show, became a breakaway hit. "Married with Children," coarse by anyone's definition, helped brand the network as edgier and younger than its network elders and prefigured some of its recent successes, such as Seth MacFarlane's animated "Family Guy."

Meanwhile, local Fox stations conjured up newscasts with a brisker, more tabloidy feel. By 1992 Murdoch decided that the local stations Fox owned and ran itself would no longer carry CNN's feed (which he had obtained from CNN founder Ted Turner at a dear cost). In 1995 Murdoch brought to New York one of his foremost British executives, Andrew Neil. To be precise, Neil was a Scot, like Murdoch's grandfather, but not stereotypically dour. The mirthful former reporter and editor for the Economist had served for nearly a dozen years as editor of Murdoch's Sunday Times; he was also the founding chairman of Sky TV, later merged into BSkyB, today one of the most important holdings the Murdochs control. Neil came to the US to help guide the creation of Fox News.

The birth of Fox News sprang from Murdoch's decision to create a television empire around sports, as he had previously in Australia and the U.K. In 1993 Fox bought the rights to broadcast the games of the NFL's then dominant NFC division, swiping football from CBS for nearly $1.6 billion. "We're a network now. Like no other sport will do, the NFL will make us into a real network," Murdoch exulted to Sports Illustrated. "In the future there will be 400 or 500 channels on cable, and ratings will be fragmented. But football on Sunday will have the same ratings, regardless of the number of channels. Football will not fragment."

He was right. And he wanted a winning weekly bookend for football to strike at another top-rated CBS program. "At that stage, Rupert Murdoch had in mind to set up a Fox News answer to '60 Minutes,'" Neil told me. "It was to be an hour-long news show going out after the NFL football program on Fox." His costar was to be Judith Regan, a young woman who had sliced her way to the top-selling echelons of the book publishing business. Smart, and possessed of finely sharpened elbows, Regan had by this point been rewarded with her own imprint, ReganBooks, at Murdoch's HarperCollins publishing house. Neil started getting uneasy as Murdoch brought in a consultant to help punch up the concept of what news would look and sound like on Fox. The idea of creating a show yielded to the idea of creating an entire cable network—a niche news channel.

The new network would speak to viewers who felt the rest of the press was too liberal, like the *New York Times*, even 60 Minutes itself. The consultant had been a political strategist for presidents Richard Nixon and George H.W. Bush, the executive producer of a TV show starring Rush Limbaugh, and the head of financial news channel CNBC.

His name was Roger Ailes.

MSNBC launched at about the same time. It was a partnership of Microsoft and the giant manufacturing and finance conglomerate GE's NBC division. In short, its executives had very little idea of what they were doing other than amortizing NBC News's costs across an additional channel. A parade of executives came and left in the ensuing decade.

Under Ailes, Fox's vision was clear and pure. Its cultural sensibility offered a modern version of a "Mad Men" world, where opinions were declarative: men were confident; professional women smart, young, and sleek. And it chased stories of dysfunction in Bill Clinton's America.

"I'll tell you what television didn't do at the time," Ailes later told Esquire magazine. "It didn't reflect what people really thought. I mean, they're sitting there saying, 'Wait a minute, New York's going broke, Los Angeles is broke, the United States is broke, everything the government has run is broke, Social Security is broke, Medicare is broke, the military is broke, why do we want these guys making all these decisions for us?'"

The American news consumer of just fifteen years ago would not have been able to recognize the country's current media landscape—the range of choices, the technological innovations, and in particular the cacophony. And no other news organization has done more in recent years to reshape that terrain than Fox. Just about every news organization either mimics or reacts against the way Fox presents the news and the values it represents.

That's not because Fox News breaks many big stories. It doesn't. (Part of the brilliance of its financial model is to have a lean reporting staff.) That's not because the channel draws the biggest audiences in news. Nor does it do so in television news, with some exceptions, though it is a dominant force in cable television.

What Fox News does, instead, is to determine what it believes should be the story of the day. It is a choice intended not just to select its own coverage, but to force others to pay attention—day after day. Fox News does so with an eye for episodes overlooked by other major news outlets. It particularly seeks storylines and themes that reflect and further stoke a sense of grievance among cultural conservatives against coastal elites.

"Cable news punches above its weight, if you look at its influence," former Fox News vice president David Rhodes once told me. "How many people are actually watching it, from moment to moment?" The highest-rated shows draw between 2.5 and 3.3 million viewers on any given night, at most a bit more than 1 percent of the US population.

When not inflamed, the channel's anchors often look as though they're having fun. And the network's news staff includes some professionals whose work could appear on any number of outlets.

At the outset, Ailes made a couple of key moves on the news side to shore up its credibility on the air. He hired John Moody, a veteran of Time magazine and United Press International (UPI), as a senior news executive. Fox's first reporters included Jon Scott and Gary Matsumoto of NBC. Catherine Crier of CNN and Court TV became an early anchor. Tammy Haddad, the executive producer and creator of CNN's "Larry King Live," was briefly employed to develop a Sunday public affairs interview show carried on both the Fox network and on the cable channel. As perhaps Washington's premier booker of top-shelf guests, Haddad also helped to plot the show's launch more generally. The first day, anchors interviewed Israeli prime minister Benjamin Netanyahu, Nation of Islam leader Louis Farrakhan, and GOP presidential candidate Bob Dole. For the desired core audience, the channel offered someone to root for, someone to root against, and someone to vote for.

On the first day, Bill O'Reilly, formerly of ABC, CBS, and the tabloid television show "Inside Edition," appeared on his new program "The O'Reilly Report" (later rechristened "The O'Reilly Factor"). "How did television news become so predictable and in

Have the Dynamics of Contemporary Media Contributed to Extremism?

some cases so boring?" O'Reilly asked viewers. "Few broadcasts take any chances these days and most are very politically correct. Well, we're going to try to be different—stimulating and a bit daring, but at the same time, responsible and fair."

Those remarks sounded much more temperate than O'Reilly proved to be. He had a calibrated sense of rights and wrongs, and a hair-trigger temper. With O'Reilly, Sean Hannity, a forceful conservative paired with a relatively weak liberal, Alan Colmes, and Bill Shine, who oversaw the opinion hosts, the new network was defined at least in part from its earliest days by three Irish Catholics from Long Island who liked a good rumble.

One of the most important new faces of Fox was Brit Hume. He had been a political reporter for the Baltimore Evening Sun and did legwork and writing for Jack Anderson's investigative column. (The CIA had briefly put Hume under surveillance after the column featured some scoops involving the agency.) He had risen to become the chief White House correspondent for ABC News. Tall and courtly, his suits often accompanied by a pocket square with a printed pattern complementing his ties, Hume bestowed credibility and class on the brash new network. His wife, Kim Hume, had left ABC to become Fox's first Washington bureau chief before he arrived.

Brit Hume was a hardworking reporter with a textured understanding of political combat and a sly appreciation for irony. He had been the one to make the considered case for the journalistic soundness of the Fox way. Most reporters and editors, he argued, approached their jobs with professionalism but could not escape a culturally liberal outlook. Reporters covered gay rights and environmental activists through this prism, Hume said, seeing parallels to the civil rights movement, and failed to subject them to the same scrutiny social and religious conservatives faced.

"A very large percentage of readers and viewers out there were really insulted and found their sensibilities offended," Hume told me some years later. "I had always had the feeling that if somebody built a broadcast network that challenged that, that there would be a remendous market for it." Stories not being told by the other news outlets represented "low-hanging fruit," the kinds of pieces that could be reported evenhandedly by anyone but were not selected for broadcast or publication elsewhere.

A push for new EPA rules might strike the Washington Post or CBS News as a story about the debate over cleaner water. Fox might frame the same story around small business owners struggling to keep pace with red tape from Washington.

Perhaps most important, Ailes instinctively recognized good television and understood how to create it—defining "good" as something viewers would want to watch and keep watching. It was close to Murdoch's definition of the public interest. In this case, Ailes knew that Fox's defining feature would require a highly cultivated resentment toward other news organizations. The "fair and balanced" slogan alone was an increasingly explicit assertion that mainstream press organizations were not fair or balanced. "We report. You decide," provoked the same reaction in viewers and the competition. On Fox, the news programs served to get out the mission statement: the other news organizations look down on you and your beliefs. Here, you're home.

Fox initially had to fight to force cable system providers to carry the network. Luckily for Ailes, he had a powerful friend in the nation's most populous metropolitan region. Time Warner's refusal to welcome Fox in New York City caused Mayor Rudolph Giuliani to threaten to carry the channel (along with Bloomberg TV) on the city's public access station. Giuliani also implied he would revoke Time Warner's lucrative cable franchise for the city. His brass-knuckled tactics showed a preference for one for-profit over another. He argued that Time Warner was favoring its own station, CNN.

Murdoch had been angered by Time Warner's roadblocks. Ailes had run Giuliani's first, unsuccessful bid for the mayoralty in 1989, and they remained close. Top Murdoch executives (including Ailes) had spoken more than two dozen times with aides at City Hall to coordinate a strategy in a two-month period.

The coordination was too cozy for the federal judge ruling on the case. "The city's purpose in acting to compel Time Warner to give Fox one of its commercial channels was to reward a friend and to further a particular viewpoint. As a consequence, Fox was the recipient of special advocacy," wrote federal judge Denise Cote. "The city has engaged in a pattern of conduct with the purpose of compelling Time Warner to alter its constitutionally protected editorial decision not to carry Fox News. The city's actions violated longstanding First Amendment principles that are the foundation of our democracy."

Yet Time Warner yielded. And Fox took advantage to build a greater audience. It covered the Clinton impeachment as ABC built "Nightline" on coverage of the Iranian hostage drama—an ongoing crisis with an uncertain outcome of national import. Only Fox News would tell the full truth, its tenor implied.

The pacing was fast, the graphics crisp and lively. Fox's Ailes wanted viewers to enjoy what they saw. And he made enough liberals part of the mix to ensure some ideological clashes. Ailes hired people he had battled during earlier political campaigns, including Geraldine Ferraro and Bob Beckel, Walter Mondale's campaign manager. Children of such prominent Democratic families as the Kennedys and the Jacksons found work at Republicans' new favorite place to watch TV.

In 2000, Fox News covered the political conventions for the first time. In news from the Middle East, Fox won favor with many Jewish viewers by employing the term "homicide bomber," rather than the more common "suicide bomber," to keep the emphasis on the deaths of innocents, not the perpetrators. Fox painted those who did not climb on board its various campaigns as opposed to the country's well-being.

Media Outlets Are Focused on Attracting Attention, Not Informing the Public

Ben Gerow

Ben Gerow is a public relations professional and writer. He is based outside Washington, DC.

In two weeks I begin my public relations career with a small firm outside of Washington D.C. Preparing for my career I've been doing a lot of research and deep thinking about public relations and how it affects the world today. One troubling trend that is impossible to avoid is the publicity that comes with being the loudest voice in the room. I'll go into examples of loud voices that have taken over our digital lives recently including Donald Trump (sorry), and LaVar Ball. This trend has also seemed to prove the theory that "There is no such thing as bad press". Conventional thought seems to disprove this thought but when looking at the (relative) Trump and Ball are having it definitely raises questions. Before diving into a debate in whether the press this trend is giving individuals is actually good press I decided to research how this trend started, and if an end is in sight.

State of Modern Media

Media has historically been dominated by TV and Newspapers. These media outlets were the gatekeepers that anyone with a story had to go through. If you wanted to promote a product, tell your story, or get anyone's attention, you had to be picked. A journalist had to pick up your story and do the work to get it into the world. It wasn't too long ago that cable and newspaper subscriptions were high and companies didn't need gimmicks to get you to read or watch. I probably won't be the first person to tell you

"Being the Loudest Voice in the Room," by Ben Gerow, Blogging The Journey, May 23, 2017. Reprinted by permission.

Have the Dynamics of Contemporary Media Contributed to Extremism?

that subscriptions for TV continue to spiral downward and the newspaper industry as we knew it, is dead.

A study in July 2016 showed that 25% of households don't pay for cable television. Another study in the same month shows that only 20% of Americans get their news from newspapers and that number lowers to 14% for the 18–29 age range. Newspapers are now being forced to put their content online and print less papers. To salvage revenues they have a paywall for their content and run an ad-based business model. This means that publishers like the Washington Post give you a certain number of articles free, but after you read enough you'll be forced to subscribe. They also sell ad space on their website to generate revenue even if you aren't subscribing.

The rise of social media has also hurt traditional media companies. By the time a newspaper is printed the content is outdated, we've already gotten the news on our social media feeds. While newspapers have historically broken stories and given deep insight, they are left now with the sole purposes of keeping the government accountable, and giving a sense of community. Social media also allows us to see "bits" from TV shows, we no longer need to watch the full program. I get sports highlights directly to my Instagram and watch Late Night with Jimmy Fallon clips on YouTube. There's no need to turn into SportsCenter every morning or stay up late and watch the full episode of Fallon.

Where does this leave us?

The major functions of television and newspapers have changed with the rise of social media. Now networks and papers rely on advertising dollars to even stay in business, and to get these dollars they need viewership. Nowhere is this more prevalent than sports talk shows where we've seen the rise of "takes". Skip Bayless has made a living saying outrageous takes to draw in viewers. We may have complained that his opinion is outrageous, but that didn't stop us from tuning in every morning to First Take. The more viewers he drew in with his outrageous takes, the more advertising dollars ESPN got. This was a big confusion during the ESPN layoffs earlier in the month. Twitter was up in arms about ESPN cutting their NHL staff and MLB writers. The thing most people don't realize from the outside is that it's a business. The amount of readers checking on ESPN's daily NHL updates fails in comparison the amount of business Stephen A. Smith brings in on a daily basis. Firing Stephen A. and keeping their NHL team would probably result in a better product, but less business, a chance a failing industry cannot take.

This also explains the presence of LaVar Ball across sports media. Even though he's made outrageous claims like beating Michael Jordan in 1 on 1, saying he wants a Billion dollar shoe deal for his kids, and making Lonzo's first pair of shoes cost $495, networks eat him up. They know that LaVar will say something outrageous that will create controversy on social media and bring in viewers. Last week he disrespected a female reporter and made fun of a fat guy, and Fox Sports couldn't have been happier because it meant people would watch and spread the story on social media.

The fact of the matter is strictly reporting the news and having mature debates won't bring in viewers, controversy will. This leads to louder voices having a bigger platform. No one took advantage of this more than our President, Donald Trump.

The Trump Effect

Months before the general election I was listening to my favorite podcast, The Tim Ferriss Show. The guest on this particular episode was Scott Adams, creator of Dilbert. The topic of Trump's media strategy came up and Scott had an interesting angle that is almost surreal in hindsight. He was predicting that Donald Trump would win the election because he was trained in persuasion and hypnosis. He said that Trump was running on emotions, not data.

> *And he bolsters that approach, Adams says, by "exploiting the business model" like an entrepreneur. In this model, which "the news industry doesn't have the ability to change … the media doesn't really have the option of ignoring the most interesting story," says Adams, contending that Trump "can always be the*

most interesting story if he has nothing to fear and nothing to lose."—Donald Trump Will Win in a Landslide

Put yourself in the shoes of a network executive. Your viewership has gone down and your job is on the line if you don't bring people in. What is more likely to catch the attention of your viewers, a new environmental policy Bernie Sanders promoted, or Donald Trump saying that John McCain wasn't a war hero because he was caught? Certainly the controversial Trump statement would lead to more debate and discussion, and give people at home a reason to post on social media.

Trump's entire campaign was run on the fact that the more outrageous things he said, the more publicity he would get, and the more people he would have talking about him. Perhaps the biggest example of this was during the first Presidential debate. Clinton was schooling him on his previous statements and lack of policies when he said "I said very tough things to [Rosie O'Donnell], and I think everybody would agree that she deserves it and nobody feels sorry for her." Guess what news stations talked about the next day? Trump's controversial comments. More press for him, less for Clinton.

The Trump Effect has trickled down to the LaVar Ball's of the world. No matter how outrageous the statement, he becomes the most interesting story. Every outlet picks it up, and more people are talking about his clothing brand.

Is There Such Thing as "Bad Press"?

This trend raises the age old question of is there such thing as bad press? History has shown that yes, there can be circumstances where the press you receive negatively impacts your brand. It's hard to argue that the oil spill was positive press for BP, they are still known for their mistake. Public scandals can ruin a celebrities image and sponsorship's, such as Tiger Woods. The opposing argument is that even with bad press, you have a platform to correct your mistake and head down a new path.

Even with winning the election because of his press coverage Trump sports an average approval rating below 40% (something

Political Extremism in the United States

that never happened to Obama). A majority of the country doesn't like him, and don't want to do business with him.

LaVar Ball may have received an extreme boost in name recognition and social media following, Adidas, Nike, and Under Armour all passed on signing his son to a sneaker deal. People are speculating on whether teams will pass on his son Lonzo to avoid dealing with him.

This leads us to a valuable lesson, attention matters, but so does trust and credibility. With the current state of media. attention is easy. Anyone can rattle off crazy statements to have their voice heard. But once you are heard, how do people feel about you? As a brand, and as a person, you should provoke a feeling of trust and credibility with your audience.

Looking Ahead

It's no surprise that the current state of TV and newspapers is not sustainable. They are dying, and they are dying fast. Unfortunately, no one has the answer for what's next for the mediums. We've entered untested waters as newspapers install paywalls and TV networks join the streaming platforms. There's no telling if the future will break the trend of loud voices dominating our devices. With the public attention Trump and LaVar Ball have received, there's one thing we can be certain of, imitators.

Even with the annoying trend just remember that attention is only one piece of the puzzle. They may have our attention, but they don't have to have our money. I urge everyone reading to get your attention organically and establish trust with your audience. We've seen short cuts pop up, but they are short lived.

Extremism and Demagoguery Emerge from Social Dynamics that Have Little to Do with Media Coverage

Larry Diamond

Larry Diamond is a senior fellow at the Hoover Institution and at the Freeman Spogli Institute for International Studies, where he directs the Center on Democracy, Development, and the Rule of Law. Diamond also serves as the Peter E. Haas Faculty Co-Director of the Haas Center for Public Service at Stanford University.

For at least half a century, the bedrock of confidence in democracy's future has been its unquestioned stability in Europe and North America. The United States and Britain survived the near-total obliteration of democracy by the fascist powers in World War II. Then the re-establishment and rapid consolidation of liberal democracies across Western Europe—and especially in Germany and Japan—laid the foundations for the global expansion of democracy that followed.

After World War II, there was only one other serious challenge to America's democratic way of life. That was the dark period in the 1950s when Senator Joseph McCarthy and his political allies launched a witch-hunt against alleged and imagined communist sympathizers that stifled civil liberties and ruined the lives of many innocent people. The McCarthy era was an ugly one, but the threat was ultimately confronted and defeated by the forthright actions of courageous Americans in the media (such as Edward R. Murrow), in politics (such as Maine Senator Margaret Chase Smith), in the law (such as chief counsel for the Army Joseph Welch), and in the judiciary (led by Supreme Court Chief Justice Earl Warren). Many of these Americans, like Smith and Warren, were from McCarthy's own Republican party.

"It Could Happen Here," by Larry Diamond, (c) 2016 The Atlantic Media Co., as first published in The Atlantic Magazine. All rights reserved. Distributed by Tribune Content Agency, LLC, October 19, 2016.

Since the reactionary fever of McCarthyism broke in America, the story of democracy in the United States has been largely one of progress, particularly the extension of rights to African Americans, Latinos, lesbians and gays, and other excluded minorities. Progress has been uneven and incomplete. It has had to confront setbacks—Watergate, post-9/11 flashes of anti-Muslim prejudice, ongoing racism in policing and the justice system, and the floodtide of dark money in politics, to name a few. But the power and example of the United States inspired and supported an unprecedented expansion of democracy globally from the mid-1970s through the early 2000s. During this period the proportion of democracies among the world's states more than doubled, and democracy became the predominant form of government in the world, with virtually all the rest of Europe, most of Latin America, half of Asia, and more than a third of African states becoming democratic. In the past decade, and especially in the past two years, freedom and democracy have been receding with the implosion of the Arab Spring and the reversals of democracy in countries like Thailand, Turkey, Bangladesh, and Nicaragua. But a majority of states in the world have remained democratic. And few have doubted the stability of democracy in the United States—until this year.

Over the decades, many scholars and writers have wondered what would happen if a demagogue like Joe McCarthy ever captured the nomination of a major political party. The scar that McCarthy left on American democracy was so deep that his name is now synonymous with the unscrupulous mobilization of fear and intolerance for extremist political ends. McCarthyism is the practice of making inflammatory, reckless, and unsubstantiated allegations about the character and patriotism of others in order to achieve political advantage. But it is not just character assassination. Neither is it ideological extremism—McCarthy had no coherent ideology. Most fundamentally, it is what Seymour Martin Lipset and Earl Raab called, half a century ago in their now once-again vital book *The Politics of Unreason*, procedural extremism. This is the antithesis of pluralism: intolerance of difference and dissent, and unwillingness to be bound by "the limits of the normative procedures which define the democratic political process." This kind of extremism treats "cleavage and ambivalence as *illegitimate*" and seeks to close down "the market place of ideas." It is what we witness when aspiring strongmen like Vladimir Putin in Russia, the late Hugo Chavez in Venezuela, Recep Tayyip Erdogan in Turkey, or—we should now deeply worry—Rodrigo Duterte in the Philippines win elections and then begin to intimidate and suffocate pluralism in the media, intellectual life, civil society, and even the business community, on the way toward one-party or one-man rule.

No political impulse could be more contrary to the founding American spirit than anti-pluralism. At its core, the American democratic experiment has been about the free contest of ideas, interests, and groups, along with tolerance for opponents and respect for their legitimacy. But throughout American history, that core principle has been challenged under social and political stress by a succession of extremist movements and politicians—the Know-Nothings, the American Protective Association, the Ku Klux Klan, Father Charles Coughlin, George Wallace, the John Birch Society. A striking common thread in these eruptions has been the interplay of ethnic, racial, and religious bigotry with jingoistic nationalism, nativist fear of foreign subversion—hence fanatical opposition to immigration—and populist animus toward educated elites, portrayed through wild conspiracy theories as plotting to betray "the people." Periodically, these have given vent to anti-Semitism by putting Jews and alleged Jewish control of banks at the heart of these imagined diabolical plots.

In his desperate bid to win the presidency, Donald Trump has increasingly embraced the rhetoric and logic of the extremist far right in American history. The elements were there for all to see from the beginning of Trump's campaign—the fanning of fears about illegal immigration, about Mexicans bringing drugs and crime, about Muslims bringing terrorism; fears of outsiders, of globalization, of difference. Trumpism is modern-day McCarthyism—stoking hysteria about treason and betrayal, fomenting ever-more outlandish theories of an establishment out to get the ordinary people that he "alone" can save, and denying the legitimacy or even decent intentions of opposing politicians. But prior to Trump no extremist movement or politician ever captured the nomination of a major political party. And none ever had the masterful command of communication media that Trump has had of television and the internet.

As a result, we now enter the final three weeks of this distressing presidential election campaign with Trump relentlessly warning that the election will be rigged, with his most vociferous surrogate, Rudy Giuliani, asserting that this will mainly happen in the "inner cities" (meaning by racial minorities), and with 41 percent of all voters (and nearly three-quarters of Republicans) agreeing that the election could be stolen from Trump. All of this is planting the seeds for a potentially traumatic and unprecedented challenge to the legitimacy of the election outcome and the new president if Trump does not win. And that is not to mention his promise to, if elected, prosecute Hillary Clinton and "lock her up," and his repeated allusions to (gun) violence as the only way that the people—betrayed by the elites—might have left to deal with Clinton as president. As the *New York Times* columnist Thomas Friedman noted in August, it was this kind of inflammatory incitement and denial of legitimacy that fed the extremist atmosphere in which Israeli Prime Minister Yitzhak Rabin was assassinated in 1995.

The history of democracy globally is strewn with examples of extremists and demagogues manipulating prejudice, insecurity, and fear in a bid for power. In this sense, Trump is nothing new. And from the Poland to the Philippines, the virus of political extremism and intolerance—of anti-pluralism—is once again spreading, placing the survival of democracy in jeopardy. Democracy has failed several times before in the Philippines, most notably in 1972, when Ferdinand Marcos, nearing the end of his second elected term as president in the midst of an armed communist insurgency, declared martial law and became a dictator. It failed once before in Poland in 1926, when Marshal Jozef Pilsudski staged a coup d'etat against a fragmented and poorly functioning party system. It was widely assumed that the rebirth of democracy after the Cold War, and its maturation in a modern and now economically successful Poland that is part of the EU, would give it immunity from reversal, but now a right-wing, anti-pluralist government is gutting constitutional constraints on its power and stifling opposition in politics as well as the media. Democratic failure could happen again in Poland—and certainly the Philippines. But could it happen here?

Among the most dangerous sins of democrats in times of trouble are arrogance and apathy. The severe polarization of American politics—to the point where Trump's support base appears to be sticking with him despite his increasingly anti-democratic statements and the mounting allegations of his sexual abuse of women—is one sign of the trouble Americans are in. Fanaticism is another. Recall Trump's statement in Nevada in February about the intensity of his support: "Sixty-eight percent would not leave [me] under any circumstance. I think that means murder. I think it means anything." Perhaps most disturbing of all are the signs that several years *before* the rise of Trump, support for democracy had begun to decline significantly, especially among young people, and not only in the US but in Europe as well.

Democracies fail when people lose faith in them and elites abandon their norms for pure political advantage. In *The Breakdown of Democratic Regimes*, the late Yale political scientist Juan Linz stressed two factors in the failure of democracy. One is the growth of "disloyal opposition"—politicians, parties, and movements that deny the legitimacy of the democratic system (and its outcomes), that are willing to use force and fraud to achieve their aims, and that are willing to curtail the constitutional rights of their political adversaries, often by depicting them as "instruments of outside secret and conspiratorial groups." But at least as great a danger, Linz warned, was "semiloyal behavior" by parties and politicians willing "to encourage, tolerate, cover up, treat leniently, excuse or justify the actions of other participants that go beyond the limits of peaceful, legitimate ... politics in a democracy." It is now not only fair but necessary to ask whether those in Donald Trump's party who fail to denounce his democratic disloyalty are not themselves doing great damage to American democracy.

In 1935, as Hitler was consolidating totalitarian rule in Germany and the demagogic Senator Huey Long was preparing to run for president in the US, Sinclair Lewis published a novel about a charismatic populist senator who is elected president by promising to restore the country to prosperity and greatness and then turns into a dictator. The title of Lewis's book was *It Can't Happen Here*. For more than half a century, Americans have blithely assumed that democracy is so rooted in their norms and institutions that nothing like that could happen here. If Americans do not renew their commitment to democracy above all partisan differences, it can.

The Media Is Beholden to the Political Forces at Play
Indira Lakshmanan

Indira Lakshmanan is the Newmark chair in journalism ethics at the Poynter Institute and a Boston Globe *columnist. She has reported from the US and 80 other countries for the* Globe, Bloomberg, *the* International New York Times, NPR, PBS, *and* Politico Magazine.

B reitbart News hit a wall Tuesday in its campaign to storm the ramparts of the media establishment when one of the most influential press associations in Washington, D.C. denied its application for credentials to cover Congress because of concerns over the site's funding, staffing, workspace and independence.

The decision by the Standing Committee of Correspondents of the House and Senate Press Gallery — a body chaired by five reporters from mainstream news outlets including Bloomberg News, The Omaha World-Herald and The Washington Post — also means the site's temporary credentials won't be renewed when they expire May 31.

It's a significant setback for the popular right-wing website that championed Donald Trump's bid for president and whose former executive chairman, Stephen Bannon, became Trump's campaign chairman and chief White House strategist.

A permanent credential would not only be Breitbart's ticket to cover hearings and roam the halls of Congress; it's also a key to other doors in the D.C. media establishment. The credential is a prerequisite to joining the White House Correspondents' Association, a membership that includes rotation in "pool duty" covering the president's activities and the right to buy tables at the prestigious annual White House Correspondents' scholarship

"Breitbart struggles to define its role in Trump era: Bad boy, watchdog or lapdog?" by Indira Lakshmanan, The Poynter Institute, April 26, 2017. Reprinted by permission.

dinner that most presidents dutifully attend (Trump is boycotting this year).

Breitbart's failed bid so far to get a Congressional press credential is part of the larger and unresolved story of how it positions itself in the Trump era. Does it remain a rebellious, naysaying outsider unconcerned with establishment trappings? Does it evolve into a more conventional partisan newsroom and formally distance itself from deep-pocketed financial backers? Or does it become a mere mouthpiece for a president it helped elect?

The latter, of course, is the most dangerous path. I spent years as a correspondent in China, a society hobbled by state-run media and the lack of a free press, and no self-respecting US news organization would want to be an organ of state power taking marching orders from 1600 Pennsylvania Avenue.

"The problem Breitbart has is a common one in journalism: How do you balance speaking truth to power and keeping access to power?" said Lee Stranahan, a former investigative journalist at Breitbart who quit a few weeks ago in a dispute over what he perceived as instructions not to ask questions at the White House press briefing about an investigation he was working on.

The balance between truth and access that Stranahan highlights is one ethical challenge his former employer faces, but it's far from the only one.

Breitbart has reveled in storming the establishment's ideological barricades since its founding a decade ago by Andrew Breitbart, the late liberal-turned-conservative publisher, critic and bête-noir of the news industry. That creation story also makes it hard to imagine the site's founder storming more literal barricades to gain admittance to the ranks of the elites he routinely derided.

The site gained fame by ginning up controversy around so-called scandals involving liberal politicians and groups, including the heavily edited hidden-camera video that purported to expose ACORN.

Waving a far-right pirate flag of politically incorrect views in a sea of largely centrist and liberal-leaning mainstream news outlets, Breitbart amassed a devoted following in a fractured media landscape years before Trump rode a populist, nationalist wave to the White House.

Before joining Trump's campaign, Bannon famously called the site "the platform for the alt-right," a term associated with White supremacists and nativists who reject mainstream conservatism and spew misogynist, racist, anti-immigrant and anti-Semitic views on social media and lately, in public.

The website has earned criticism for publishing such incendiary headlines as: "The solution to online 'harassment' is simple: Women should log off," "Bill Kristol: Republican spoiler, renegade Jew," "Birth control makes women unattractive and crazy," "There's no hiring bias against women in tech, they just suck at interviews," and "Hoist it high and proud: The Confederate flag proclaims a glorious heritage."

Stories like these have sparked outrage from critics in the media and beyond. Sleeping Giants, a Twitter campaign that began last year, is pressuring advertisers to boycott racist and sexist media, and claims more than 1,900 brands, including Kellogg's, BMW and Visa, have pulled ads from Breitbart. Employees at Amazon are pressuring management to stop their ads from appearing on Breitbart through algorithms that buy ads from third-party advertising exchanges.

Despite the controversy, Breitbart's following pushed the site's traffic to 17.3 million unique visitors in January 2017, up from 14.1 million a year earlier, according to comScore. Alexa ranks Breitbart the 64th most popular site in the US, while SimilarWeb ranks it 122 among all news and media sites globally. It continues to build its social media following and currently boasts 3.36 million likes and 686,000 followers on Facebook and Twitter, respectively.

Now that Breitbart's chosen candidate is ensconced in the Oval Office, its insurgent outsider status is changing. It's sought some of the trappings and recognition of insider status, including congressional and White House credentials, coveted interviews with key officials and a seat at the table alongside mainstream media outlets that Breitbart and its ideological fellow travelers dismissively refer to as "the MSM." They've recently hired journalists from a couple of those traditional outlets, The Hill and The Wall Street Journal, to build expertise and sourcing.

"They want to be seen as the outlet of record in the Trump era, they want to be taken seriously," said Oliver Darcy, a media reporter formerly with Business Insider who has covered Breitbart.

But aside from scoops doled out to favored outlets by the White House (an Oval Office interview with Trump, an exclusive Facebook livestream with Press Secretary Sean Spicer) and the occasional invitation to prestigious panels as the representative of alt-right media, keeping up with the Joneses has proved difficult.

Breitbart was given the opportunity to be part of White House press pool coverage on Inauguration Day, but it was limited to "supplemental" pool duty, which usually means the Vice President's or First Lady's schedule, not the presidential pool rotation that's set by the White House Correspondents' Association.

The Trump White House has been generous with Breitbart, as one might expect, given the site's unwavering support for the president's candidacy and Bannon's current perch. Entry to the briefing room is granted by the White House, not the Correspondents' Association, and Breitbart and other partisan outlets are well-represented and often called on for questions.

But that attention hasn't always worked out well for Breitbart, said Will Sommer, campaign editor at The Hill and author of the Right Richter newsletter that covers right-wing media.

The Facebook livestream with Spicer was "astonishingly badly produced, like a weird horror movie," Sommer said. "They got a big break and blew it. And [Washington Editor] Matt Boyle had this giant Oval Office opportunity to interview Trump, and his questions were like, 'Mr. Trump, why is the media so bad?'"

"They're trying to use this moment to mainstream themselves and professionalize their operation, and they want the signifiers of legitimacy," he added. Whether they're going to get the legitimacy is something else. That only comes with exposing your financial arrangements."

Phone calls, voicemail messages and repeated emails to Breitbart's CEO and general counsel Larry Solov, its Washington editor Matt Boyle and its spokesman Chad Wilkinson were not returned Tuesday.

In a statement provided to other media, Wilkinson said Breitbart is "unequivocally entitled to permanent Senate Press Gallery credentials and is determined to secure them," without elaborating on how the site plans to do that.

Senate Press Gallery committee members say Breitbart is wrong to presume it is "entitled" to a credential simply because it's a news organization, and wrong if they assume they were denied for ideological reasons. The issue, the correspondents say, is an irregular operation, a lack of transparency and the failure to prove editorial independence from funders and political activists, despite stating that a prominent donor has no editorial involvement.

The standing committee of correspondents has been policing the independence of members and issuing credentials for more than 130 years, according to its website. Senate Press Gallery Director Laura Lytle points to article 4 of its rules: applicants must not be engaged in lobbying or paid advocacy, nor have any claim before Congress or the federal government. The rules further state: "publications must be editorially independent of any institution, foundation or interest group that lobbies the federal government, or that is not principally a general news organization."

This is where things get dicey for Breitbart, which is partially owned by Robert Mercer, a billionaire hedge fund manager and far-right donor, and his daughter Rebekah. The Mercers also fund the Government Accountability Institute, a nonprofit research institute co-founded by Bannon, which bought ads on Breitbart's site and handsomely compensated three top officials who were simultaneously on the news site's payroll: Bannon, Peter Schweizer and Wynton Hall, according to a Washington Post investigation.

GAI's political advocacy work has raised questions about its tax status as a public charity.

Breitbart provided conflicting dates of employment for Bannon, who stepped down from Breitbart before becoming Trump's chief strategist, and for Hall, who worked for GAI and Breitbart at the same time, according to the correspondents' committee. Breitbart's Solov wrote that Hall resigned as managing editor, but media reporter Darcy says his sources say Hall is still "very involved," signing onto Breitbart's Slack channel and assigning stories.

The standing committee insists this is not about the establishment locking arms against Breitbart over its far-right views. Other conservative digital upstarts have been approved for credentials, including The Daily Caller, co-founded by Fox News host Tucker Carlson. And liberal and left-wing outlets tied to advocacy groups, including Media Matters, a media watchdog that belongs to a progressive research group, and ThinkProgress, a site that belongs to the liberal Center for American Progress, have failed to get credentials, according to committee records.

Even SCOTUSblog, a nonpartisan site dedicated to the Supreme Court that has won many journalism awards, wasn't granted credentials because it's run by lawyers, not by a news organization, standing committee chairman Billy House, a correspondent for Bloomberg (and former colleague of mine), told me.

White House Correspondents' Association president and Reuters correspondent Jeff Mason refused to confirm whether any Breitbart reporters are members. WHCA currently requires journalists to obtain a congressional credential to join, but some members who got a congressional pass and WHCA membership while working for another outlet may have maintained membership after moving to Breitbart.

Questions were raised last month when a writer for the Daily Signal, a news and commentary site for the Heritage Foundation, a conservative think tank that has a sister political action committee, filed a White House pool report. Mason said it was supplemental pool duty covering the Vice President, not the President's regular pool rotation that's for members only, but criteria for all pools is now being reviewed, along with membership bylaws.

Senate Press Gallery committee chairman House said the door's still open for Breitbart to cut ties to advocacy groups, eliminate perceived conflicts of interest and obtain credentials. But since the site put in its bid last year, House said a series of letters about its masthead, ownership, staffing, links to advocacy groups and commercial address in a single-person residence raised more questions than they answered.

House acknowledged that media owners may have political leanings, but they can't interfere with news gathering for those to be independent media. Former New York Mayor and Bloomberg LP founder Mike Bloomberg, billionaire investor Warren Buffett and Amazon.com and Washington Post owner Jeff Bezos all own news organizations represented on the standing committee. "Owners can have opinions, but here has to be a firewall between their activities and editorial operations," House said.

Stranahan, the former Breitbart journalist, argues that the old-school journalism gospel that reporting can't be tied to money from advocacy groups is an outdated tenet for an era when the news business is struggling to survive.

"A lot of new media outlets — whether it's [left-wing] Amy Goodman and 'Democracy Now' or whoever are funded by outside political interest groups because the economic bottom fell out of journalism some years ago with the internet," said Stranahan, who now has a radio show for the Russian government-funded Sputnik news agency. He sees no problem with going from far-right media to Russian funding because he says no restrictions are being put on his work.

"That's the problem for everyone in journalism now — how do you make money? We need to revisit that assumption" that journalism can't have political ties. "That's the illusion of objectivity that establishment media has been attempting to promote, and I don't agree. You can't tell me The New York Times doesn't have a political agenda or that Jeff Bezos doesn't have political interests," said Stranahan, who has a podcast called "Making the News."

Stranahan would welcome all comers, as long as they're transparent about their interests and funders. Don't expect Media Matters, which has taken funding from liberal billionaire George Soros, to do a hit piece on Soros, he says, and don't expect Breitbart to do a hard-hitting take on the Mercers.

He is critical of Breitbart for what he sees as blind devotion to Trump, for abandoning a jaundiced eye for critiquing power. But he says the argument that editors are taking direct orders from the White House is bunk.

But do calls come in? Stranahan argues that just because Bannon joined the White House, he shouldn't be barred from criticizing coverage he thinks is erroneous.

Stranahan's argument works only so far. A politician has a right to protest false or unfair reporting, but the words of a former media boss and are very likely to influence coverage in a way that's improper once they're in public office.

There's one piece of Stranahan's advice for his former employer that I heartily endorse: Aside from being transparent about your funding and associations, he suggests getting an ombudsman to monitor the site's reporting and content from the inside, to communicate with readers on the outside and to keep a critical eye so it doesn't become a state media mouthpiece. Setting aside all its other issues, a site that started as a bête noir doesn't want to end up any president's lapdog.

CHAPTER 4

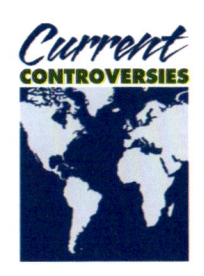

Has the Internet and Its Growing Role in Society Contributed to Political Extremism?

The Power of Social Media and the Internet Has Created Opportunities and Perils for Society

Clay Shirky

Clay Shirky is an American writer, consultant, and educator on the social and economic effects of internet technologies and journalism.

On January 17, 2001, during the impeachment trial of Philippine President Joseph Estrada, loyalists in the Philippine Congress voted to set aside key evidence against him. Less than two hours after the decision was announced, thousands of Filipinos, angry that their corrupt president might be let off the hook, converged on Epifanio de los Santos avenue, a major crossroads in Manila. The protest was arranged, in part, by forwarded text messages reading, "Go 2 EDSA. Wear blk." The crowd quickly swelled, and in the next few days, over a million people arrived, choking traffic in downtown Manila.

The public's ability to coordinate such a massive and rapid response—close to seven million text messages were sent that week—so alarmed the country's legislators that they reversed course and allowed the evidence to be presented. Estrada's fate was sealed; by January 20, he was gone. The event marked the first time that social media had helped force out a national leader. Estrada himself blamed "the text-messaging generation" for his downfall.

Since the rise of the Internet in the early 1990s, the world's networked population has grown from the low millions to the low billions. Over the same period, social media have become a fact of life for civil society worldwide, involving may actors—regular citizens, activists, nongovernmental organizations, telecommunications firms, software providers, governments. This raises an obvious question for the US government: How does the

"The Political Power of Social Media," by Clay Shirky, Council on Foreign Relations, January - February 2011. Reprinted by permission.

ubiquity of social media affect US interests, and how should US policy respond to it?

As the communications landscape gets denser, more complex, and more participatory, the networked population is gaining greater access to information, more opportunities to engage in public speech, and an enhanced ability to undertake collective action. In the political arena, as the protests in Manila demonstrated, these increased freedoms can help loosely coordinated publics demand change.

The Philippine strategy has been adopted many times since. In some cases, the protesters ultimately succeeded, as in Spain in 2004, when demonstrations organized by text messaging led to the quick ouster of Spanish Prime Minister José María Aznar, who had inaccurately blamed the Madrid transit bombings on Basque separatists. The Communist Party lost power in Moldova in 2009 when massive protests coordinated in part by text message, Facebook, and Twitter broke out over and obviously fraudulent elections. Around the world, the Catholic Church has faced lawsuits over its harboring of child rapists, a process that started when *The Boston Globe*'s 2002 exposé of sexual abuse in the church went viral online in a matter of hours.

There are, however, many examples of the activists failing, as in Belarus in March 2006, when street protests (arranged in part by e-mail) against President Aleksandr Lukashenko's alleged vote rigging swelled, then faltered, leaving Lukashenko more determined than ever to control social media. During the June 2009 uprising of the Green Movement in Iran, activists used every possible technological coordinating tool to protest the miscount of votes for Mir Hossein Mousavi but were ultimately brought to heel by a violent crackdown. The Red Shirt uprising in Thailand in 2010 followed a similar but quicker path: protesters savvy with social media occupied downtown Bangkok until the Thai government dispersed the protesters, killing dozens.

The use of social media tools—text messaging, e-mail, photo sharing, social networking, and the like—does not have a single preordained outcome. Therefore, attempts to outline their effects on political action are too often reduced to dueling anecdotes. If you regard the failure of the Belarusian protests to oust Lukashenko as paradigmatic, you will regard the Moldovan experience as an outlier, and vice versa. Empirical work on the subject is also hard to come by, in part because these tools are so new and in part because relevant examples are so rare. The safest characterization of recent quantitative attempts to answer the question, Do digital tools enhance democracy? (such as those by Jacob Groshek and Philip Howard) is that these tools probably do not hurt in the short run and might help in the long run—and that they have the most dramatic effects in states where a public sphere already constrains the actions of the government.

Despite this mixed record, social media have become coordinating tools for nearly all of the world's political movements, just as most of the world's authoritarian governments (and, alarmingly, an increasing number of democratic ones) are trying to limit access to it. In response, the US State Department has committed itself to "Internet freedom" as a specific policy aim. Arguing for the rights of people to use the Internet freely is an appropriate policy for the United States, both because it aligns with the strategic goal of strengthening civil society worldwide and because it resonates with American beliefs about freedom of expression. But attempts to yoke the idea of Internet freedom to short-term goals—particularly ones that are country-specific or are intended to help particular dissident groups or encourage regime change—are likely to be ineffective on average. And when they fail, the consequences can be serious.

Although the story of Estrada's ouster and other similar events have led observers to focus on the power of mass protests to topple governments, the potential of social media lies mainly in their support of civil society and the public sphere—change measured in years and decades rather than weeks or months. The US government should maintain Internet freedom as a goal to be pursued in a principled and regime-neutral fashion, not as a tool for effecting immediate policy aims country by country. It should likewise assume that progress will be incremental and, unsurprisingly, slowest in the most authoritarian regimes.

The Perils of Internet Freedom

In January 2010, US Secretary of State Hillary Clinton outlined how the United States would promote Internet freedom abroad. She emphasized several kinds of freedom, including the freedom to access information (such as the ability to use Wikipedia and Google inside Iran), the freedom of ordinary citizens to produce their own social media (such as the rights of Burmese activists to blog), and the freedom of citizens to converse with one another (such as the Chinese public's capacity to use instant messaging without interference).

Most notably, Clinton announced funding for the development of tools designed to reopen access to the Internet in countries that restrict it. This "instrumental" approach to Internet freedom concentrates on preventing states from censoring outside Web sites, such as Google, YouTube, or that of *The New York Times*. It focuses only secondarily on public speech by citizens and least of all on private or social uses of digital media. According to this vision, Washington can and should deliver rapid, directed responses to censorship by authoritarian regimes.

The instrumental view is politically appealing, action-oriented, and almost certainly wrong. It overestimates the value of broadcast media while underestimating the value of media that allow citizens to communicate privately among themselves. It overestimates the value of access to information, particularly information hosted in the West, while underestimating the value of tools for local coordination. And it overestimates the importance of computers while underestimating the importance of simpler tools, such as cell phones.

The instrumental approach can also be dangerous. Consider the debacle around the proposed censorship-circumvention software known as Haystack, which, according to its developer, was meant to be a "one-to-one match for how the [Iranian] regime implements censorship." The tool was widely praised in Washington; the US government even granted it an export license. But the program was never carefully vetted, and when security experts examined it, it turned out that it not only failed at its goal of hiding messages from governments but also made it, in the words of one analyst, "possible for an adversary to specifically pinpoint individual users." In contrast, one of the most successful anti-censorship software programs, Freegate, has received little support from the United States, partly because of ordinary bureaucratic delays and partly because the US government is wary of damaging US-Chinese relations: the tool was originally created by Falun Gong, the spiritual movement that the Chinese government has called "an evil cult." The challenges of Freegate and Haystack demonstrate how difficult it is to weaponize social media to pursue country-specific and near-term policy goals.

New media conducive to fostering participation can indeed increase the freedoms Clinton outlined, just as the printing press, the postal service, the telegraph, and the telephone did before. One complaint about the idea of new media as a political force is that most people simply use these tools for commerce, social life, or self-distraction, but this is common to all forms of media. Far more people in the 1500s were reading erotic novels than Martin Luther's "Ninety-five Theses," and far more people before the American Revolution were reading *Poor Richard's Almanack* than the work of the Committees of Correspondence. But these political works still had an enormous political effect.

Just as Luther adopted the newly practical printing press to protest against the Catholic Church, and the American revolutionaries synchronized their beliefs using the postal service that Benjamin Franklin had designed, today's dissident movements will use any means possible to frame their views and coordinate their actions; it would be impossible to describe the Moldovan Communist Party's loss of Parliament after the 2009 elections without discussing the use of cell phones and online tools by its opponents to mobilize. Authoritarian governments stifle communication among their citizens because they fear, correctly, that a better-coordinated populace would constrain their ability to act without oversight.

Despite this basic truth—that communicative freedom is good for political freedom—the instrumental mode of Internet statecraft is still problematic. It is difficult for outsiders to understand the local conditions of dissent. External support runs the risk of tainting even peaceful opposition as being directedd by foreign elements. Dissidents can be exposed by the unintended effects of novel tools. A government's demands for Internet freedom abroad can vary from country to country, depending on the importance of the relationship, leading to cynicism about its motives.

The more promising way to think about social media is as long-term tools that can strengthen civil society and the public sphere. In contrast to the instrumental view of Internet freedom, this can be called the "environmental" view. According to this conception, positive changes in the life of a country, including pro-democratic regime change, follow, rather than precede, the development of a strong public sphere. This is not to say that popular movements will not successfully use these tools to discipline or even oust their governments, but rather than US attempts to direct such uses are likely to do more harm than good. Considered in this light, Internet freedom is a long game, to be conceived of and supported not as a separate agenda but merely as an important input to the more fundamental political freedoms.

[…]

The Rapid, 24/7 News Cycle Made Possible by Modern Media Technology Has Diminished the Depth and Quality of Public Discourse

Ben Harack

Ben Harack is a writer at Live to Learn *and the founder of the blogs* Vision of Earth *and* Condensed Matters.

The advent of intense media speed and opinion masquerading as news have had some damaging effects on our political system. This is especially evident in the coverage leading up to and during elections. We now have horse-race reporting on elections, where we spend more time talking about who has the lead and who is catching up. We hear about the status of the polls more than the global and nation-shaping issues that form the platforms of the candidates.

We tend to hear fewer of the once notorious journalistic questions with regards to governmental action. The media just ends up parroting the government with regards to what is going on. Rosenberg and Feldman accuse the news media of being relatively uncritical and asking few questions when George W. Bush announced that the United States had been victorious in the Iraq war. Commenting on the Iraq war, Arianna Huffington said that "media watchdogs acted more like lapdogs."

Fewer Questions, More Answers

The business of political journalism has become less about asking tough questions and more about being the first to announce what the government recently did. Also, reporting is generally interpreted through the political lens of whatever organization publishing it. Fox is republican, MSNBC is democrat, and CNN pushes their own agendas.

"Media speed's negative effect on politics," by Ben Harack, COPYRIGHT 2010 BEN HARACK ALL RIGHTS RESERVED, Vision of Earth, October 17, 2010. Reprinted by permission.

Trivializing Political Debate

In their book *No Time to Think*, Rosenberg and Feldman mention that debates at the time of Abraham Lincoln were often 60-90 minutes per speaker. Today our televised debates often have 60-90 seconds for discussion of issues of tremendous scope and complexity. In No Time to Think, Rosenberg and Feldman quote an example from the trivialized debates of this day and age:

> "What would you do, in the eyes of Muslims, to repair America's image? Mayor Giuliani – 90 seconds." – Anderson Cooper during CNN-Youtube GOP candidate debate on Nov 29th, 2007.
>
> "How do you repair the image of America in the Muslim world? – 30 seconds to respond." – Cooper asking another candidate to respond to Giuliani.

How can we even begin to discuss issues of this magnitude in such time frames? Of course we can't. The fact is, these political 'debates' are far more a media and popularity gimmick than a tool for understanding how we can shape the fate of our society. News media get lots of content they can feed the beast with, and political candidates get a chance to score points against their opponents in these brief clashes.

Rosenberg and Feldman ask the critical question: What do sound bites and rapid speech debates have to do with the candidate's ability to govern? Not much, I'd say. 'Political debates' seem better oriented to help us select good actors, speakers, and entertainers.

Rosenberg and Feldman also claim that media speed also makes it harder for governments to actually be honest and straightforward with their people. It is easier for governments to hire people to answer the media with empty rhetoric along party lines.

Pressure on Decisions

The lightning speed of news puts pressure on political figures to make faster decisions. In the case of most crises today, a very significant portion of the population is likely to be made aware of the crisis within hours or days. With the populace becoming more accustomed to increased speed of information and action, they would be putting pressure on the government to act quickly.

The problem is that acting quickly can be acting rashly. We do not want media pressure to push our governments into doing terrible things. I believe that we cannot afford guesswork and hype regarding the most important issues facing our society.

Rosenberg and Feldman tell a scary story. They interviewed Ted Sorensen, an important advisor to John F. Kennedy during the Cuban Missile Crisis. Sorensen, a person who is generally an optimist, is convinced that if there had been significant media pressure on the government to act early in the Cuban Missile crisis, it would have led to a preemptive strike against soviet forces who were armed with nuclear weapons and authorized to use them. His opinion is that this action would have escalated to a full nuclear exchange, ending civilization as we know it.

The stakes are high, and we can't afford to let our media put undue pressure on our governments to act quickly. On the other hand, we can't let our governments get away with not listening to us or answering our questions. Our media, to some extent, is a reflection of what we are thinking about and what we are feeling. If our government finds that they only way they can make decent decisions is to tune out the media, we are heading down a scary path.

Who Has the Credibility to Question Government?

It used to be that journalists were the ones who would ask the tough questions of government. They could be relied upon to demand answers of government, and they were well-respected enough that the government would hesitate to ignore them. They were not called media watchdogs for nothing. Who watched the watchers? Their editors, other media companies and media forms, and the people. Our news media today is all-too-often acting for profit, not for the public interest. They ask fewer questions but shout out more answers.

With regards to journalism in general, Rosenberg and Feldman say that "When your independence goes, so does your integrity." If you as a journalist have the job of increasing advertisement productivity, selling products, or increasing viewership, you have lost a critical portion of your credibility. Our news media today is serving corporate interests that damage their ability to contribute meaningfully to discussion and investigation of real issues.

Social Media and the Internet Have Failed to Mitigate Persistent Class-Based Gaps in Political Participation

Marc Hooghe, Jennifer Oser, and Sofie Marien

Marc Hooghe is affiliated with the University of Leuven in Belgium. Jennifer Oser is an affiliate of Ben-Gurion University. Sofie Marien is affiliated with the University of Amsterdam.

In every election cycle, news stories tout the potential of online activism to engage people who have historically been less engaged in offline politics — particularly young people, women, and people with less education and income. Could this be true? If so, there would be new possibilities for enlarging American democracy — in an age when 1 in 3 eligible US adults skips voting in presidential elections and two-thirds of potential voters fail to show up in midterm elections.

But what if online activism mainly offers ways for citizens who are regularly politically active offline to amplify their already loud voices? In that case, online political opportunities would largely reinforce existing political inequalities.

Using national data on Americans who engage in various types of online and offline political participation, our research examines the evidence about these competing "new mobilization" and "reinforcement" perspectives on the impact of online activism.

Who Participates Online?

We start by noting the percentage of the US population engaged in various kinds of online and offline political activities, using data from a 2008 Pew Survey that asked a national sample of

"Does the Internet help more Americans become politically active?" Scholars Strategy Network, November, 29, 2015. https://journalistsresource.org/studies/politics/citizen-action/internet-online-political-active. Licensed under CC BY-ND 4.0 International.

Americans whether they had performed each act at any point in the previous 12 months.

Probing further, we used a novel statistical technique called latent analysis to see whether some people are especially active online but not very politically active offline. Then we compared the characteristics of online activists to those of other kinds of participants.

Four Types of Political Participants

In our data, we find four distinctive types of participants.

- Online specialists: About 8 percent of Americans constitute a relatively small group of citizens who are especially active online, involved in activities such as online petitioning and joining an online political group.
- Offline specialists: 9 percent of the US adult population primarily engage in offline political activities such as demonstrating and being an active member of an organization that tries to influence policy.
- Contact specialists: Another 10 percent of Americans engage both online and offline in contacting activities, ranging from contacting a government official in person to emailing a national official about an issue of personal importance.
- Disengaged people: 73 percent of the US adult population is relatively unlikely to vote or engage in any other sort of political activity either online or offline.

No Simple Technological Corrective for Class Gaps

Can those who hope for broader and more equal participation in American democracy take new heart from recent trends, including the spread of online activism? There are some hopeful tendencies in our data. Although research since the 1960s indicates that older men tend to be the most politically active, in our 2008 data we found that women are just as politically active as men. We also find that young people have become highly active in online forms of political engagement.

But our findings contain discouraging news about persistent class gaps, because online political activity in 2008 largely reinforces longstanding inequalities in political participation. Compared to Americans with lower levels of income and educational attainment, Americans with higher incomes and educational attainment are much more likely to be politically active both online and offline. These findings are just a snapshot in time — but they suggest that the advent of new technological possibilities for online political activism has not, to date, become any kind of magic cure for participatory inequalities in US political and civic life.

In the years ahead, online political activism is likely to evolve more swiftly than offline activism. But evolving forms of online engagement could simply increase the leverage of people who already have many participatory tools at their disposal. Anyone who hopes that the Internet will readily draw millions of previously unengaged Americans into the political process should realize that, even though online activists are increasingly likely to include young people and women, they may very well continue to be wealthier and better educated than most of the US population.

Confirmation Bias Threatens the Potential Benefits of a Diverse Media Environment

Martin Maximino

Martin Maximino is managing partner of the i4 Group. He holds a Master's degree in public policy from Harvard University's John F. Kennedy School of Government.

From health care reform and global warming to marijuana legalization and same-sex marriage, voters are increasingly polarized, particularly along partisan lines. In this context, the level of fragmentation in the media landscape is assumed to be an important explanation for this polarization.

While the impact of the media on political beliefs and preferences is undeniable, the extent to which media affect voters' choices and partisanship is still under study. In the era of "big broadcast," prior to the Internet, scholars were concerned about the lack of media diversity and the fact that citizens were a "captive audience" potentially subject to mass manipulation. Thus, many hoped that the democratization of news media, particularly online, could have a positive impact on political participation, civic engagement and the production of information. However, in a digital era featuring media abundance, scholars now worry about what they call "selective exposure." A more fragmented media environment may prompt citizens to seek out more like-minded news sources, contributing to the reinforcement of prior beliefs and opinions and exacerbating polarization. Thus, an "echo chamber" — Fox News and MSNBC are often cited as examples — can make certain views even louder and more pronounced among a group of like-minded individuals. These media dynamics are thought to

---

"Does media fragmentation contribute to polarization? Evidence from lab experiments," by Martin Maximino, Journalist's Resource, August 22, 2014. https://journalistsresource.org/studies/society/news-media/media-fragmentation-political-polarization-lab-experiments. Licensed under CC BY-ND 4.0 International.

be at work as we witness shifts in public opinion on topics such as climate change.

Behind this debate is a fundamental cognitive truth established by the behavioral science field: The majority of individuals have a confirmation bias. When individuals are open to evaluating arguments for a certain position, they are likely to be constrained by cognitive biases that make them reinforce their initial position, even in the presence of contradictory evidence.

A 2014 study in *Public Opinion Quarterly*, "The Informational Basis for Mass Polarization," analyzes the effects of individuals' information environment on opinion dynamics and the role of prior attitudes in moderating those effects. To study whether information choice serves as a foundation for polarization, the author, Thomas Leefer of Aarhus University, conducted two experiments in Northwestern University's Political Science Research Laboratory involving information choice behavior at the micro-level on health care reform and US military action in Libya. The experiments involved 176 undergraduates in the first study, while the second study involved a mix of students and Internet-recruited non-students, totaling 300 persons. The experimental procedures provided informational prompts and gave subjects the chance to search through and read different kinds of articles — constituting the "information environment," and a way of "priming" subjects — before asking them about their views on the issues.

The study's finding include:

- Individuals reacted to the information environment by choosing more articles or news in the direction of the slant of the environment. Individuals in "pro" environments — in favor of a particular position — read more pro than con arguments; those in mixed environments also read more pro than con articles; those in con environments read the same number of pro and con articles.
- Individuals' opinions moved in the direction of the slant of the environment. On a scale from 0 to 1, the information

environment was found to make a difference of 0.04 in opinions — the equivalent of 4 percentage points.
- However, the role of high- and low- importance beliefs — those who have strong, dogmatic beliefs on a subject, versus those with little preconceived opinion — is key to understanding the link between search behavior, opinions, and information environment.
- Regardless of the fragmentation of the media environment in the experiment, individuals with high-importance attitudes became more polarized toward their initial position. This is because they appear to evaluate information in a consistent way, regardless of the information they encounter. On the other hand, low-importance respondents' opinions did not change much and actually moved in a similar fashion to a control group that was not subject to manipulations.
- A pro-slanted environment makes individuals more supportive over time. However, the size of that effect will be highly conditional on the importance of prior attitudes: Individuals with low-importance prior attitudes will be more affected by the relative fragmentation of the media compared to those with strong attitudes.

"The results presented here suggest that information choice, at least among those with personally important opinions, does not appear to make those individuals or democracy better off," Leefer concludes. "Freedom to choose one's political news seemed to many scholars of the 1980s a much-needed component of democratic health, but the abundance of choice that has emerged in the 'post-broadcast' present is now being seen as democratically problematic.... This paper has shown that the implications of choice are highly conditional." The experimental evidence suggests that "polarization therefore seems to require more than media fragmentation," and therefore may be better explained by deeper societal patterns.

Related Research

A 2013 study published in *Public Opinion Quarterly*, "Extreme Groups: Interest Groups and the Misrepresentation of Issue Publics," looks to empirical evidence to help settle some of these debates, testing whether members of motivated groups are "giving voice" to wider public communities or pushing their own unrepresentative agendas. Also of interest is a 2013 study published in *Psychological Science*, "Political Extremism Is Supported by an Illusion of Understanding," that explores a central paradox of our politically polarized era: How can people maintain such strong views on complex policy issues that they seldom understand with any sophistication? The researchers attempt to measure the degree of overconfidence people typically have in their own understanding of the mechanics of how systems and issues work, and to evaluate how the process of explaining their views might moderate extremism.

Citizens Who Consume More Media Are More Politically Engaged
John Wihbey

John Wihbey is an assistant professor of journalism and new media at Northeastern University, where he serves as the faculty graduate programs advisor, an instructor in the Media Innovation program, and a faculty affiliate with the NULab for Texts, Maps, and Networks.

Academic research has consistently found that people who consume more news media have a greater probability of being civically and politically engaged across a variety of measures. In an era when the public's time and attention is increasingly directed toward platforms such as Facebook and Twitter, scholars are seeking to evaluate the still-emerging relationship between social media use and public engagement. The Obama presidential campaigns in 2008 and 2012 and the Arab Spring in 2011 catalyzed interest in networked digital connectivity and political action, but the data remain far from conclusive.

The largest and perhaps best-known inquiry into this issue so far is a 2012 study published in the journal *Nature*, "A 61-Million-Person Experiment in Social Influence and Political Mobilization," which suggested that messages on users' Facebook feeds could significantly influence voting patterns. The study data — analyzed in collaboration with Facebook data scientists — suggested that certain messages promoted by friends "increased turnout directly by about 60,000 voters and indirectly through social contagion by another 280,000 voters, for a total of 340,000 additional votes." Close friends with real-world ties were found to be much more influential than casual online acquaintances. (Following the study,

"How does social media use influence political participation and civic engagement? A meta-analysis," by John Wihbey, Journalist's Resource, October 18, 2015. https://journalistsresource.org/studies/politics/digital-democracy/social-media-influence-politics-participation-engagement-meta-analysis. Licensed under CC BY-ND 4.0 International.

concerns were raised about the potential manipulation of users and "digital gerrymandering.")

There are now thousands of studies on the effects of social networking sites (SNS) on offline behavior, but isolating common themes is not easy. Researchers often use unique datasets, ask different questions and measure a range of outcomes. However, a 2015 metastudy in the journal *Information, Communication & Society*, "Social Media Use and Participation: A Meta-analysis of Current Research," analyzes 36 studies on the relationship between SNS use and everything from civic engagement broadly speaking to tangible actions such as voting and protesting. Some focus on youth populations, others on SNS use in countries outside the United States. Within these 36 studies, there were 170 separate "coefficients" — different factors potentially correlated with SNS use. The author, Shelley Boulianne of Grant MacEwan University (Canada), notes that the studies are all based on self-reported surveys, with the number of respondents ranging from 250 to more than 1,500. Twenty studies were conducted between 2008 and 2011, while eight were from 2012-2013.

The study's key findings include:

- Among all of the factors examined, 82% showed a positive relationship between SNS use and some form of civic or political engagement or participation. Still, only half of the relationships found were statistically significant. The strongest effects could be seen in studies that randomly sampled youth populations.
- The correlation between social-media use and election-campaign participation "seems weak based on the set of studies analyzed," while the relationship with civic engagement is generally stronger.
- Further, "Measuring participation as protest activities is more likely to produce a positive effect, but the coefficients are not more likely to be statistically significant compared to other measures of participation." Also, within the area of protest activities, many different kinds of activities — marches,

demonstrations, petitions and boycotts — are combined in research, making conclusions less valid. When studies do isolate and separate out these activities, these studies generally show that "social media plays a positive role in citizens' participation."
- Overall, the data cast doubt on whether SNS use "causes" strong effects and is truly "transformative." Because few studies employ an experimental design, where researchers could compare a treatment group with a control group, it is difficult to claim causality.

"Popular discourse has focused on the use of social media by the Obama campaigns," Boulianne concludes. "While these campaigns may have revolutionized aspects of election campaigning online, such as gathering donations, the metadata provide little evidence that the social media aspects of the campaigns were successful in changing people's levels of participation. In other words, the greater use of social media did not affect people's likelihood of voting or participating in the campaign."

It is worth noting that many studies in this area take social media use as the starting point or "independent variable," and therefore cannot rule out that some "deeper" cause — political interest, for example — is the reason people might engage in SNS use in the first place. Further, some researchers see SNS use as a form of participation and engagement in and of itself, helping to shape public narratives and understanding of public affairs.

Social Media Offers New Tools for Political Engagement

Deana A. Rohlinger

Deana A. Rohlinger is a professor of sociology and Associate Dean for Faculty Development and Community Engagement at Florida State University. Her research focuses on mass media, political participation, and politics in America.

Virtual petitions, online money-bombs, forums to debate issues, and the use of social media and email to recruit people for meetings and protests – all are ways in which today's political activists try to engage citizens and influence the political process. Social movements across the political spectrum use new technologies to effect change and influence party politics, but little is systematically known about how they do it – or what difference it makes.

A recent study looked closely at MoveOn and Tea Party activists in Tallahassee, Florida. On the progressive side, MoveOn participants are part of a centralized web-based organization that encourages local activists to host events as part of nationwide campaigns. On the conservative side, Tea Party activism is nationwide but not centrally managed. Grassroots Tea Party groups have formed in localities, including three in Tallahassee. In addition to doing participant observation and analyzing media coverage, websites, and public documents, researchers did in-depth interviews with MoveOn and Tea Party activists to gain fresh insights into how they use various forms of internet-based communication to pursue their political goals. The results show how social movements operate in the internet age. By acting nimbly outside established organizational channels, successful social

"How Social Movements are Using the Internet to Change Politics," by Deana A. Rohlinger, Scholars Strategy Network, January 2012. http://www.scholarsstrategynetwork.org/brief/how-social-movements-are-using-internet-change-politics. Licensed under CC BY-ND 4.0 International.

movements have brought the "entrepreneurial spirit" online and into the American political system.

Internet Technologies Overcome Obstacles to Participation

- Online groups overcome well-known obstacles to participation – such as time constraints, lack of skills, and low income. Online movements let people choose when to click; and they usually do not charge membership dues in any traditional sense. They encourage participation in lots of small ways – allowing people to share opinions, sign petitions, ask to be kept informed, and donate small amounts of money.
- Successful online groups use internet communications and networking to teach supporters new political skills and get them involved in the "real world." Models for action can be rapidly disseminated, and people can be given tools to get in touch with other potential supporters in their community. Supporters can be taught how to host political gatherings, organize a rally, and canvass their neighbors online.
- Effective groups use technology to get supporters involved in the decision-making process – for example, by hosting forums for discussion or by asking people to give their opinion about issues to highlight. This sustains support for a cause, because individuals see the organization as democratic and responsive to their feedback.

Internet Tactics Help Movements Stress Big Ideas and Downplay Controversy

Rather than promoting specialized causes or detailed platforms, technologically savvy political activists focus on selling big ideas that promise to change the world, stressing themes that unify rather than divide citizens from many different backgrounds.

- Movements use the internet along with other approaches to push messages that pit "average Americans" against

power holders such as "the party establishment" or "elite Washington insiders." For example, both MoveOn and the Tea Party portray themselves as insurgents and use strong rhetorical oppositions. The internet lends itself to any movement that wants to portray itself as going around or rebelling against elites.
- Successful social movements avoid issues that might divide supporters. Movements featuring online communication can manage what gets featured in their message. For example, MoveOn uses internet feedback to find high priorities that unite supporters, and it also learns what might divide people and reduce enthusiasm. Similarly, Tallahassee Tea Party groups avoid highlighting abortion and gay marriage – "hot button" issues that create fissures among their supporters.

Social Movements and Political Parties

The ability of social movements to leverage internet communication technologies with great effectiveness changes dynamics between movements and political parties in the 21st century. Internet-savvy movements can help fill in gaps in party structures. For example, in recent elections progressive groups like MoveOn.org have targeted swing states with campaigns designed to bring progressive voters to the polls on behalf of Democrats. And Tea Party groups spread enthusiasm among Republican voters in 2010. But at the same time, social movements use the internet to pressure and compete with the major political parties. This happens in several ways:

- Social movements draw dollars away from political parties. Political parties must struggle to represent voters on many issues, while raising money and maintaining broad support. Yet internet savvy social movements operating outside of direct party control can sometimes use a sharper message to raise millions and get supporters involved beyond the checkbook. This may diminish the fundraising ability of political parties. Small and big donors alike turn to activist

groups they believe can quickly and effectively challenge established politicians and policy positions.
- Savvy movements can use advertising, earned media, and viral campaigns to build support for their issues and force political parties to take up their causes. For example, since 2009 all Republican candidates and officeholders have scrambled to address Tea Party calls for cuts in spending and reductions in the national debt. Movements have always pressured parties, but movements in the internet era can have a big impact very quickly.
- Movement activists believe that attempts to establish a third party will fail, and so they pressure and work with the closest major party. Tea Partiers, for example, pressure Republicans and compete for party leadership positions at local, state, and national levels; and MoveOn participants support Democrats who favor movement stances on key issues.

Organizations to Contact

The editors have compiled the following list of organizations concerned with the issues debated in this book. The descriptions are derived from materials provided by the organizations. All have publications or information available for interested readers. This list was compiled on the date of publication of the present volume; the information provided here may change. Be aware that many organizations take several weeks or longer to respond to inquiries, so allow as much time as possible.

The Centrist Project
2420 17th St.; 3rd Floor
Denver, CO 80202
phone: (703) 962-1354
email: campaign@centristproject.org
website: www.centristproject.org

The Centrist Project is a grassroots organization dedicated to organizing centrist Americans, supporting centrist policies, and encouraging more independent candidates to run for public office and to put national interests ahead of any political faction in order to solve problems.

Convergence Center for Policy Resolution
1133 19th Street, NW
Suite 410
Washington, DC 20036
phone: (202) 830-2310
email: info@convergencepolicy.org
website: www.convergencepolicy.org

Convergence Center for Policy Resolution is a 501(c)(3) nonprofit organization focused on solving social challenges through collaboration. The Convergence team brings deep knowledge of policy and process and works with leaders and doers to move past divergent views to identify workable solutions to seemingly intractable issues.

Democratic National Committee
430 South Capitol St. SE
Washington, DC 20003
phone: (202) 863-8000
website: www.democrats.org

Since 1848, the Democratic National Committee has been the home of the Democratic Party, the oldest continuing party in the United States.

FactCheck.org
Annenberg Public Policy Center
202 S. 36th St.
Philadelphia, PA 19104-3806
phone: (215) 898-9400
email: editor@factcheck.org
website: www.factcheck.org

FactCheck.org is a nonpartisan, nonprofit "consumer advocate" for voters that aims to reduce the level of deception and confusion in US politics. They monitor the factual accuracy of what is said by major US political players in the form of TV ads, debates, speeches, interviews, and news releases.

Fairness and Accuracy in Reporting (FAIR)
124 W. 30th Street, Suite 201
New York, NY 10001
phone: (212) 633-6700
email: fair@fair.org
website: www.fair.org

FAIR, the national media watch group, has been offering well-documented criticism of media bias and censorship since 1986.

Independent Voter Project
PO Box 34431
San Diego, CA 92163
phone: (619) 207-4618
email: contact@independentvoterproject.org
website: www.independentvoterproject.org

The Independent Voter Project (IVP) is a nonprofit, nonpartisan 501(c)(4) organization dedicated to better informing voters about important public policy issues and to encouraging nonpartisan voters to participate in the electoral process.

Pew Research Center
1615 L St. NW, Suite 800
Washington, DC 20003
phone: (202) 419-4300
website: www.pewresearch.org

The Pew Research Center is a nonpartisan fact tank that informs the public about the issues, attitudes, and trends shaping the world. It conducts public opinion polling, demographic research, media content analysis, and other empirical social science research. Pew Research Center does not take policy positions.

PolitiFact
1100 Connecticut Ave. NW
Suite 440
Washington, DC 20036
phone: (202) 463-0571
website: www.politifact.com/

PolitiFact is a fact-checking website that rates the accuracy of claims by elected officials and others who speak up in American politics.

Reason

1747 Connecticut Ave., NW
Washington, DC 20009
phone: (202) 986-0916
website: www.reason.com

Reason is the monthly print magazine of "free minds and free markets." It covers politics, culture, and ideas through a provocative mix of news, analysis, commentary, and reviews. *Reason* provides a refreshing alternative to right-wing and left-wing opinion magazines by making a principled case for liberty and individual choice in all areas of human activity.

Republican National Committee

310 First Street SE
Washington, DC 20003
phone: (202) 863-8500
website: www.gop.com

The Republican National Committee is a US political committee that provides national leadership for the Republican Party of the United States.

Southern Poverty Law Center

400 Washington Avenue
Montgomery, AL 36104
phone: (334) 956-8200
website: www.splcenter.org

The Southern Poverty Law Center monitors hate groups and other extremists throughout the US and exposes their activities to law enforcement agencies, the media, and the public.

Bibliography

Books

John Avlon. *Wingnuts: Extremism in the Age of Obama.* New York, NY: Beast Books, 2010.

Martin Durham. *White Rage: The Extreme Right and American Politics.* New York, NY: Routledge, 2007.

Jeff Flake. *Conscience of a Conservative: A Rejection of Destructive Politics and a Return to Principle.* New York, NY: Random House, 2017.

David Frum. *Trumpocracy: The Corruption of the American Republic.* New York, NY: HarperCollins, 2018.

Jonathan Haidt. *The Righteous Mind: Why Good People Are Divided by Politics and Religion.* New York, NY: Vintage Books, 2012.

John Kasich. *Two Paths: America Divided or United.* New York, NY: Thomas Dunne Books, 2017.

Matthew Levendusky. *How Partisan Media Polarize America.* Chicago, IL: University of Chicago Press, 2013.

Mike Lofgren. *The Party Is Over: How Republicans Went Crazy, Democrats Became Useless, and the Middle Class Got Shafted.* New York, NY: Penguin Books, 2012.

Thomas E. Mann and Norman J. Ornstein. *It's Even Worse Than It Looks: How the American Constitutional System Collided with the New Politics of Extremism.* Philadelphia, PA: Basic Books, 2012.

Darren Mulloy. *American Extremism: History, Politics, and the Militia Movement (Routledge Studies in Extremism and Democracy).* New York, NY: Routledge, 2004.

David Neiwert. *Alt-America: The Rise of the Radical Right in the Age of Trump.* New York, NY: Verso, 2017.

Greg Orman. *A Declaration of Independents: How We Can Break the Two-Party Stranglehold and Restore the American Dream.* Austin, TX: Greenleaf Book Group Press, 2016.

Gabriel Sherman. *The Loudest Voice in the Room: How the Brilliant, Bombastic Roger Ailes Built FOX News – and Divided a Country.* New York, NY: Random House, 2014.

Charles J. Sykes. *How the Right Lost Its Mind.* New York, NY: St. Martin's Press, 2017.

Charles Wheelan. *The Centrist Manifesto.* New York, NY: W.W. Norton & Company, Inc, 2013.

Periodicals and Internet Sources

Matthew A. Baum and Tim Groeling, "New Media and the Polarization of American Political Discourse." *Political Communication.* 2008. https://sites.hks.harvard.edu/fs/mbaum/documents/BaumGroeling_NewMedia.pdf

Russell Berman, "What's the Answer to Political Polarization in the U.S.?" *Atlantic.* March 8, 2016. https://www.theatlantic.com/politics/archive/2016/03/whats-the-answer-to-political-polarization/470163/

Nate Cohn, "Polarization Is Dividing American Society, Not Just Politics." *New York Times.* June 12, 2014. https://www.nytimes.com/2014/06/12/upshot/polarization-is-dividing-american-society-not-just-politics.html

Justin Curtis, "A Fake America: Cultural Fragmentation and Polarization." *Harvard Political Review.* January 15, 2017. http://harvardpolitics.com/online/fake-america-cultural-fragmentation-polarization/

Brett Edkins, "Report: U.S. Media Among Most Polarized In The World." *Forbes.* June 27, 2017. https://www.forbes.com/sites/brettedkins/2017/06/27/u-s-media-among-most-polarized-in-the-world-study-finds/#6c810c122546

David French, "On Extremism, Left and White." *National Review.* May 30, 2017. http://www.nationalreview.com/article/448108/political-extremism-beleaguers-both-left-and-right

Joshua Hersh, "Extremism Experts Are Starting to Worry About the Left." *Vice News.* June 15, 2017. https://news.vice.com/en_ca/article/3kpeb9/extremism-experts-are-starting-to-worry-about-the-left

Amanda Hess, "How to Escape Your Political Bubble for a Clearer View." *New York Times.* March 3, 2017. https://www.nytimes.com/2017/03/03/arts/the-battle-over-your-political-bubble.html

Michael Kazin, "A Kind Word for Ted Cruz: America Was Built on Extremism." *New Republic.* October 29, 2013. https://newrepublic.

com/article/115399/history-american-extremism-how-unpopular-opinions-became-mainstrea

Ed Kilgore, "In the Trump Era, America Is Racing Toward Peak Polarization." *New York Magazine*. May 31, 2017. http://nymag.com/daily/intelligencer/2017/05/in-the-trump-era-america-is-racing-toward-peak-polarization.html

Christopher McConnell, Yotam Margalit, Neil Malhotra, and Matthew Levendusky, "Research: Political Polarization Is Changing How Americans Work and Shop." *Harvard Business Review*. May 19, 2017. https://hbr.org/2017/05/research-political-polarization-is-changing-how-americans-work-and-shop

Pew Research Center, "Political Polarization, 1994-2017." Pew Research Center. October 20, 2017. http://www.people-press.org/interactives/political-polarization-1994-2017/

Jessica Rettig, "The Rise of Political Extremism and the Decline of Decency." *U.S. News*. April 8, 2010. https://www.usnews.com/opinion/articles/2010/04/08/the-rise-of-political-extremism-and-the-decline-of-decency

Andrew Soergel, "Is Social Media to Blame for Political Polarization in America?" *U.S. News*. March 20, 2017. https://www.usnews.com/news/articles/2017-03-20/is-social-media-to-blame-for-political-polarization-in-america

Kenneth T. Walsh, "Polarization Deepens in American Politics." *U.S. News*. October 3, 2017. https://www.usnews.com/news/ken-walshs-washington/articles/2017-10-03/polarization-deepens-in-american-politics

Index

A

abortion, 21, 47, 48, 58, 60, 62, 63, 67, 68, 186
Abramowitz, Alan, 62, 113, 114
Affordable Care Act, 31
African Americans, 25, 32, 110, 150
Ailes, Roger, 139, 140, 142, 143
American Broadcasting Company (ABC), 140, 141, 143
American Political Science Association (APSA), 20, 21
anarchists, 32
Atkinson, Michael, 92–98

B

Baldassarri, Delia, 56–75
Ball, LaVar, 144, 146–148
Béland, Daniel, 92–98
Boulianne, Shelley, 182, 183
Breitbart News, 131, 134, 155, 156–162
Brookings Center for Middle East Policy, 34, 37

C

Cable News Network (CNN), 128, 129, 132, 138, 140, 142, 170, 171
campaigning, 16, 45–47, 49–52, 183
Canada, 85–87, 94, 97, 98, 105, 182
Cascadia, 82, 85, 88
Center for Public Justice (CPJ), 35–38
climate change, 76–81, 178
Clinton, Hillary, 147, 152, 167, 168
Columbia Broadcasting System (CBS), 81, 128, 130, 138, 140, 142
communicative action theory, 39, 40, 42, 43
confirmation bias, 17, 79, 177–180
conflict, 21, 24, 39, 56, 57, 64, 70, 79, 100, 110, 124, 132, 133, 160, 161
Congress, 20, 22, 23, 28, 31, 60, 61, 77, 81, 87, 88, 90, 94–96, 108, 114, 129, 155, 159, 164
consensus, 11, 39–44, 62, 90, 100
conservatives, 21, 52, 62, 64, 67, 86, 87, 89, 111, 123, 128, 140, 141
Constitution, US, 26, 28, 32, 87, 93, 95, 99, 100, 101, 107, 121, 122, 143, 153

credibility, 80, 81, 93, 94, 133, 140, 141, 148, 172, 173
Cruz, Ted, 22, 32, 117
culture, 31, 32, 50, 104, 106, 109, 110, 114, 115, 118

D

Debs, Eugene, 32, 33
deliberation, 39–44, 100, 120
democracy, 11, 12, 13, 17, 21, 39–44, 45–52, 56, 88, 90, 94, 99–118, 119–125, 149, 150, 152–154, 166, 174, 175
Democracy Web, 119–125
Democrats, 20–22, 24, 25, 31, 32, 39, 42, 60–68, 71, 73, 78, 81, 85, 87, 89, 108, 111, 113, 114, 123, 153, 186, 187
Diamond, Larry, 149–154
discourse, 11, 39, 41–43, 132, 170, 183
diversity, 12, 16, 17, 24, 26, 51, 63, 82, 84, 97, 121, 131, 134, 177
Dunleavy, Steve, 136, 137

E

Eberhard, Kristin, 82–91
economics, 12, 16, 22, 23, 25, 42, 60, 63, 64, 66, 71, 73, 83–85, 90, 119, 123, 153, 161

Enlightenment, 40
ethics, 11, 39, 41, 156
European Union (EU), 35, 36, 153

F

Facebook, 37, 134, 157, 158, 165, 181
Federalists, 107, 120, 121
Fernandez, Alberto, 35
Ferrell, Robert E., 39–44
Finlayson, James Gordon, 41
Folkenflik, David, 136–143
Fox News, 92, 96, 128, 129, 132, 136–143, 146, 160, 170, 177
fragmentation, 98, 101–103, 104, 133, 138, 153, 177, 179
freedom of expression, 34–38, 166

G

Gelman, Andrew, 56–75
Gerow, Ben, 144–148
gerrymandering, 26–29, 88, 89, 112, 182
Global Network Initiative, 37
Gutmann, Amy, 16, 45–55

H

Habermas, Jürgen, 39–43
Harack, Ben, 170–173
Hepworth, Shelley, 131–135

Index

Hooghe, Marc, 174–176
House of Representatives, 26, 28, 92, 95
Hume, Brit, 141

I

ideology, 15, 44, 58, 59, 61, 63–65, 71, 79, 111, 123, 150
Independents, 20, 49, 77, 81, 82, 84, 85, 88, 90, 120
Internet, 26, 35, 36, 96, 133, 152, 161, 164–169, 174–176, 177, 178, 184–187
Islamic State, 34–38

J

journalists, 36–38, 131, 133, 134, 137, 144, 156, 158, 160, 161, 172, 173

L

Lakshmanan, Indira, 155–162
Leaders' Summit on Countering Violent Extremism, 34
liberals, 52, 62, 64, 68, 71, 84, 87, 111, 123, 128, 143
Libertarians, 21
Lichtenberg, Judith, 37
Lumen Learning, 20–30

M

Marien, Sofie, 174–176
Marin, Carol, 128, 130
Maximino, Martin, 177–180
McCarty, Nolan, 28, 73
Mill, John Stuart, 119, 120
millennials, 82
moderates, 15, 20, 21, 28, 52, 60, 116
Murdoch, Rupert, 136–138, 142

N

National Broadcasting Company (NBC), 128, 139, 140, 170, 177
National Public Radio (NPR), 132
New Zealand, 85, 86

O

Obama, Barack, 23, 31, 34, 35, 36, 47, 48, 49, 67, 94, 95, 181, 183
Occupy Wall Street, 22, 23
Old, Joe, 39–44
O'Reilly, Bill, 130, 140, 141
Organization for Security and Co-operation in Europe (OSCE), 35, 38
Oser, Jennifer, 174–176

P

Pew Research Center, 81, 83, 114, 174
Pildes, Richard H., 15, 99–118
pluralism, 56, 57, 65, 70, 150–152
Political Action Committee (PAC), 116
political science, 28, 45, 78, 153, 178
populism, 83–86, 89, 104, 151, 154, 157
privatization, 37, 92, 95
progressives, 82–84, 87–89, 160, 184, 186
proportional representation, 85–89, 105, 121, 122

R

Radsch, Courtney, 34–38
redistricting, 26–29, 111, 112
reform, 47, 48, 52, 86–88, 93, 98, 100–104, 107, 108, 112, 119, 124, 177, 178
Republicans, 20, 22, 24, 25, 31, 32, 42, 49, 60–64, 66, 67, 71, 73, 76–80, 85, 89, 92, 95, 111, 113, 114, 116, 143, 187
Reynolds v. Simms, 27
rhetoric, 12, 16, 36, 42, 128, 151, 171
Rohlinger, Deana A., 184–187
Ryan, Paul, 92

S

Sanders, Bernie, 22, 23, 82–85, 87, 88, 90, 91, 147
Senate, 28, 31, 35, 95, 102, 104, 111, 155, 159, 161
Shirky, Clay, 164–169
Slack, Alex, 128–130
socialists, 32, 84, 123
social media, 145, 146, 147, 148, 157, 164–169, 174–176, 181–183, 184–187
social networking sites (SNS), 182, 183
Sommer, Will, 131, 135, 158
Spooner, Lysander, 32
Stern, Ken, 132, 134, 135
Supreme Court, 26, 27, 104, 111, 160

T

Tea Party, 21–23, 92, 93, 95, 96, 184, 186, 187
Thompson, Dennis, 45–53
Thornburg v. Gingles, 111
Time Warner, 142, 143
Trump, Donald, 82–85, 87, 88, 90, 91, 132–135, 144, 146–148, 151–158, 160, 162
Twitter, 36, 37, 146, 157, 165, 181

U

United Kingdom (UK), 85, 121, 122

V

Vietnam War, 26, 33
voters, 20–24, 28, 47, 48, 59, 62, 63, 66, 71–75, 82–91, 105, 107, 110, 111, 114, 116, 117, 120, 121, 124, 132, 134, 152, 174, 177, 181, 186
Voting Rights Act, 110, 111

W

Warren, Elizabeth, 22, 117
White House Correspondents' Association, 155, 158, 160
Whitney, Trevor, 31–33
Wihbey, John, 181–183

Y

YouTube, 35, 96, 145, 167

Z

Zhou, Jack, 76–81